The Greatest Fairy Tales

by Charles Perrault,
Hans Christian Andersen
and the Brothers Grimm

Illustrations by FRANCESCA ROSSI

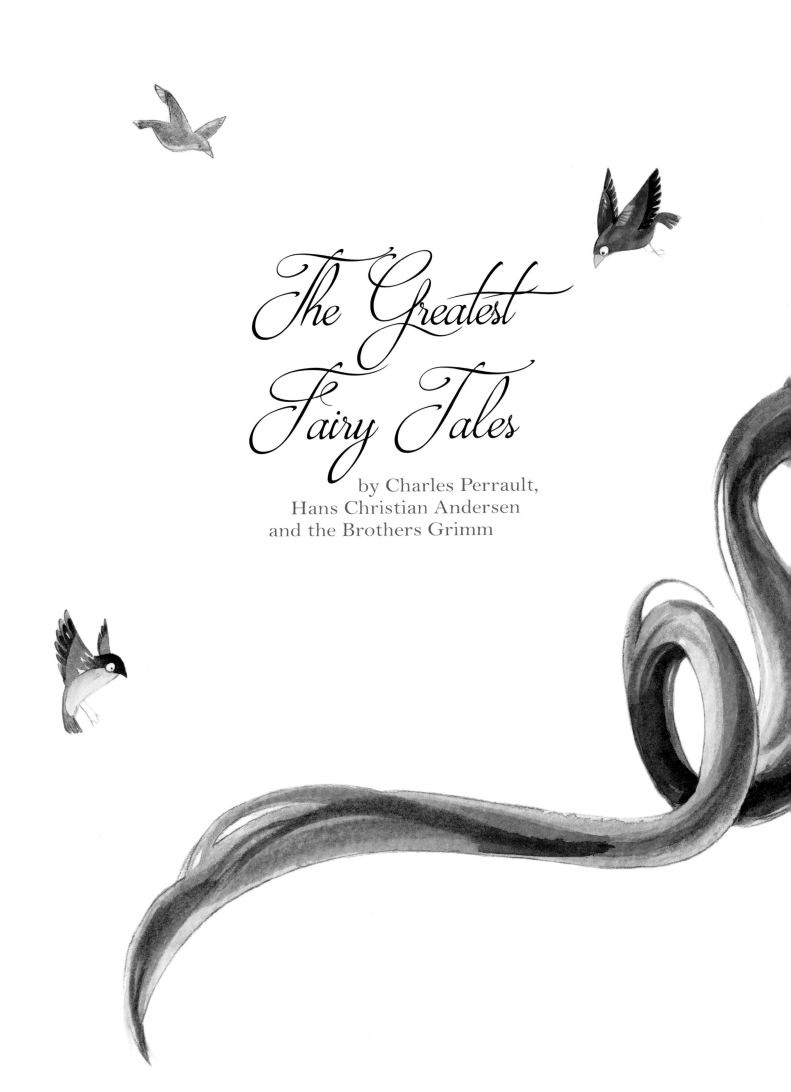

The Greatest Fairy Tales

by Charles Perrault,
Hans Christian Andersen
and the Brothers Grimm

Contents

Fairy Tales by the Brothers Grimm

Fairy Tales by Charles Perrault

Fairy Tales by Hans Christian Andersen

Introduction

The fairy-tale world is a world of enchantment, where magic spells and other wonders turn characters' lives upside down: a lovelorn prince might be hiding behind a frog's gaze; the forests are inhabited by animals by turns ruthless and sly or friendly and kind… but always clever and lively!

It's a world where princesses face countless misadventures and suffer grievous wrongs before finally finding happiness, aided by brave knights riding swiftly on their steeds to defeat fierce dragons and cruel sorcerers in the hopes of making their dreams of love come true.

Such a world may seem light years away from our everyday life, yet for centuries it's been the ideal place to lose ourselves whenever we want to dream of new adventures alongside the unforgettable characters who've been entertaining boys and girls – and countless grownups! – since the dawn of time.

The Brothers Grimm

The origins and authors of the most famous European fairy tales may be lost in the mists of time, but we have Jacob and Wilhelm Grimm to thank for collecting these stories and handing them down to posterity.

The two brothers, who lived in Germany over two centuries ago, spent decades travelling around the German countryside to collect and transcribe the stories that grandmothers would tell their grandchildren… the very stories they used to hear from their own grandmothers when they were little.

Thus, the Brothers Grimm collected over two hundred folktales, publishing them in their two 19th-century volumes!

Among them, we find unforgettable characters such as Cinderella, Hansel and Gretel, Snow White, Little Red Riding Hood and…

Turn the pages to find all the many fantastic tales that have made it down to us thanks to the tireless Brothers Grimm!

The Frog Prince

Long ago, in a faraway land, there was a king who lived in a wealthy castle with his beloved daughters.

The daughters were all beautiful, but the youngest was so lovely that even the sun was dazzled whenever it caressed her face!

The castle was surrounded by a leafy garden, at the center of which there was a pond. During the hottest hours of the day, the princess sought shelter under the trees, where she often played with a golden ball. One day, with a throw that was stronger than usual, the precious ball landed into the water and sank to the bottom of the pond. The princess was furious for having lost her favorite pastime and cried desperately. But then, just as she resigned herself to wading through the pond to retrieve her ball, she heard a hoarse voice: "I can help you, if you wish!" Surprised, the princess turned in the direction of the voice and saw a frog sitting on a water lily.

"Here is your ball: I will return it to you if you make me a promise."

Eager to get the ball back and without even thinking it over, the princess blurted out: "I'll give you anything: jewelry, gemstones, gold and silver!" The frog sat quietly, then he said: "I don't want any of those things. Promise me that you'll take me with you to the palace. I get very lonely here all on my own! I want to be at the palace and sit with you at the table, dance with you, play with you, and sleep in your bed. If you promise to care for me, to be my friend and to always stay with me, I will give you your ball." The princess thought that she would never share her bed with a frog, but she promised the frog everything he asked, just to get back her ball. As soon as he returned it, the princess laughed and ran back to the palace, quickly forgetting the incident.

A few hours later, during dinner, there was a strange sound: hop, hop, hop... It was the frog climbing the great staircase, he jumped one step at a time until he reached the king's table. The princess laughed and told her father what happened in the garden that morning, she remembered the silly promise she made to quickly and easily get her golden ball back. The king listened quietly then, with a stern expression on his face, turned to his beloved daughter and said: "Promises must always be kept; just because you are a princess doesn't excuse you from your commitments." Thus the girl was bound to keep her word.

The frog requested to be placed on the table and allowed to eat from the princess' gold plate. The girl agreed, but was unable to touch any of her food. The prospect of having to spend the entire evening with this unwanted guest filled her with dread. What could a beautiful princess ever have in common with a revolting frog?

To her great surprise, the frog turned out to be very charming: he told her amusing stories that made her burst into laughter, and he listened to her secret thoughts and dreams without judgment; thus, the princess had a wonderful evening. When it was time to go to sleep, the frog reminded the princess of the promise that he could sleep next to her in her bed, under pure linen sheets embroidered with gold. The princess was horrified: how could she sleep next to a slimy frog?

And when the frog requested a goodnight kiss, the princess became so exasperated that she rudely replied: "Oh, no! I am never going to kiss you; my lips will never get close to your disgusting mouth!"

The frog was so hurt by those cruel words that his yellow eyes filled with tears. With two leaps, he jumped onto the windowsill determined to leap back to the pond and forever leave behind the one who had so deeply humiliated him.

Only then did the princess realize just how cruel and superficial she had been: after all, had she not enjoyed the frog's company all evening?

Had they not laughed and joked like old friends?

And had she not confided in him unlike anyone before, revealing her innermost fears, insecurities and worries?

And had he not been the most understanding and sensitive of all people she had known until then?

To her great surprise she realized that she was thinking of the little frog as if he were a person, a sincere and trusted friend that she had now hurt.

Glowing with shame, she gave a long sigh and approached the frog. "Wait!" she said, "That was really rude of me. I acted foolishly and without thinking. I don't understand why you would care so much about someone like me, but if you still want a kiss, do come closer."

The frog turned to look at her with his calm and kind eyes and for a moment, the princess thought she could see him smiling.

Gently, she took him in her hands and pressed her lips against the frog's cold skin without feeling disgust or embarrassment.

A light wind tangled her long and beautiful hair, while a sweet, distant melody began playing all around.

The princess felt enveloped by a strange feeling that was calm and reassuring: slowly she opened her eyes and looked at her little friend, but what she saw, left her without words.

The frog was floating before her, in a whirlwind of golden sparks gleaming with magic light!

When all this ceased, instead of the frog there was a charming prince!

The girl was bewildered, hesitant and a little fearful, but the young man's gaze was loving and reassuring. He tenderly took her hand in his and began telling her his sad story. A long time ago, an evil and jealous witch had cast a spell on him, condemning him to live under the guise of a frog until he was kissed by a girl. At last, thanks to her, the spell had been broken and the prince was free to return to his home. As in all the best fairy tales, he asked the princess if she would take him as her husband and, with another kiss, she gave him her answer.

Rapunzel

In a small village surrounded by fields, there lived a man called Nicolas and his young wife, Anna. For many years they had dreamt of having a baby, but with no luck. Then one day their wish was finally granted.

When she was alone, Anna looked out of the window and sighed. It was a beautiful spring day and she longed to go outside. "I wish I had a garden like that," she said, looking at their neighbor's garden, which was full of all sorts of wonderful flowers and plants. "I would cook those delicious-looking vegetables!"

Their elderly neighbor spent all her time tending to her garden. In the village it was rumored that she was a witch, who used spells and potions to grow magical plants – and indeed, a witch she was.

Anna thought the rapunzel looked especially delicious. The more she looked at it, the more she wanted some. So when Nicolas came home she said, "You wanted to give me a surprise for dinner. Well, I would like some rapunzel, please!"

"Where will I find that?" said Nicolas.

"There, in our neighbor's garden," she said, pointing.

"You want me to sneak into the garden of that witch? What if she catches me?" Nicolas replied.

"Well, don't get caught!" said his wife.

That night, Nicolas climbed over the wall that surrounded their neighbor's garden and, very slowly, he made his way to the vegetable patch. After collecting a handful of rapunzel, he hurried home, shut the door behind him with relief, and said to his wife, "I've done it! I am never going back into that garden again!"

But maybe the rapunzel really was bewitched, because after tasting the delicious leaves, Anna refused to eat anything else. She fasted for days until she became ill.

Nicolas was desperate, and in the end he decided he had to sneak back into the neighbor's garden. However, he was not so lucky this time. As he was returning home, his arms full of rapunzel, he met the old witch. Nicolas shook with fear.

"I . . . I am sorry! They are for my wife," Nicolas stammered. "She is expecting a baby and refuses to eat anything other than rapunzel. She is ill and I am very worried about her!" he continued.

The old woman pointed a skeletal finger at him and said, "She may have the rapunzel, but only on one condition!"

"Anything!" said Nicolas, desperate to get away.

"When your daughter is born, you must give her to me!" she said.

Nicolas was speechless! Give their long awaited baby to this woman in exchange for some rapunzel? It was ridiculous!

But Nicolas needed to get home. He would think of what to do later. So he said, "I . . . I promise you."

Satisfied, the old woman stepped aside and Nicolas fled.

On returning home he told Anna what had happened, but she just smiled. "The old woman was joking! She wanted to scare you and she certainly managed that!" Nicolas thought his wife must be right, and they both forgot the incident.

Several months later a beautiful baby girl was born, and she occupied their every thought.

After a few years, however, the old woman knocked on their door.

Nicolas and Anna tried to hide the little girl, but the witch raised her stick and, whispering a spell, managed to take the girl from her mother's arms and vanished with her. Nobody knew where they had gone.

The witch named the child Rapunzel, and took her to a far-off land. Together they lived in a small house hidden deep in the forest. Only a few travellers ever visited those parts and the witch told everyone she was the child's grandmother, and the girl had been orphaned in a tragic accident. She said the same thing to little Rapunzel, who never doubted her words.

The witch became very fond of the girl. She showed her the kindness and the love of a real grandmother. She let her help mix potions and revealed to her the secrets for growing lush flowers and delicious vegetables. The only thing she did not allow her to do was stray too far from the house. She was very protective of the girl, and was so afraid of losing her that she forbade her to talk to anyone.

The years went by quickly and the child grew into a beautiful girl with long, golden hair. The witch decided to lock her inside a tower that was hidden by trees and

completely surrounded by a thick, thorny hedge. Using a magic spell the witch made the stairs and the entrance to the tower disappear: the only opening that remained was a tiny window. Whenever the witch wanted to climb inside, she cried: "Rapunzel let down your hair, so that I may climb up to you." The poor girl spent the days alone and, unhappy about her sad fate, consoled herself by singing, which was her only joy.

One day a prince went by and, attracted by the girl's melodious voice, he approached the tower. When he saw the girl at the window, he immediately fell in love with her.

He searched for the door to the tower so he could reach her, but finally he had to give up as there was no door to be found. He soon realized that the poor young woman was imprisoned in the tower – no one could enter, nor could she escape.

Just then he heard footsteps and he quickly hid. From behind a tree, he saw an old woman making her way to the tower. Once there, she clapped her hands and shouted, "Rapunzel, Rapunzel, let down your hair!"

She had done this every day since she had been imprisoned in the tower. The witch grabbed hold of the hair, climbed up to the window and went into the tower.

A little while later, the prince saw the witch leave the same way that she had got in – using Rapunzel's long hair as a rope.

When he was sure that she had gone, he walked over to the tower and cried, "Rapunzel, Rapunzel, let down your hair."

At first she did not recognize the prince and she was very frightened and tried to hide, but when Rapunzel heard his gentle voice, and saw his kind eyes, she welcomed the prince. By now, Rapunzel had learned that the old woman was not really her grandmother, but a witch, who had taken Rapunzel from her parents when she was young. She told the prince that the witch didn't want Rapunzel to leave her, and so had kept her prisoner in the tower.

"I'll help you escape. I'll take you to the other side of the world, if need be, so she cannot find you," promised the prince. The two of them spent the rest of the night

talking and at dawn, the prince slid down her long hair, stopping in the clearing to blow her a kiss. At that moment the witch came out of the forest and saw him.

Once the prince had gone, the witch walked over to the tower and called to Rapunzel as usual. She raised her stick, then softly whispered a spell. Immediately Rapunzel fell to the ground, asleep. Picking up a large pair of scissors, the witch cut off her long hair, and tied it tightly to the window.

She then cast a spell to make a long spiral staircase that led out of the tower. She hoisted the sleeping girl down the stairs and to a nearby cave. The witch placed Rapunzel on the ground, and then found a large rock which she dragged across the entrance to the cave. At sunset, the prince came to the tower as promised, and called out to Rapunzel to help him climb up. The witch threw down Rapunzel's hair, and waited for him. The prince turned and came face to face with the witch.

"Where is she?" he said. "Where's Rapunzel?"

"She is imprisoned in a cave in the forest, where you will never find her." The witch raised her stick and began whispering a spell, and as the prince jumped back to avoid the spell, he fell through the window and into the spiny hedge below. He was battered and bruised, but he did not seem to be badly hurt. But when he opened his eyes, he discovered to his horror that the witch had managed to cast a spell on him after all – he was blind! He stumbled to his feet,

and heard the witch scream, "You may still be alive, but you'll never find out where Rapunzel is!"

After several hours, he heard the sound of sweet singing; he followed the music, and came to a cave, the entrance of which was blocked by a large rock. He realized that this was where Rapunzel was and called to her. Working together, they managed to move the rock and Rapunzel, finally free, threw herself into the prince's arms. When she saw what the witch had done to the prince, Rapunzel began to cry. Her tears fell on the prince's eyes, and broke the evil spell, so the prince was able to see again. However, the witch saw them from the tower; she picked up her stick and pointed at the bush below, casting a spell on it to turn it into a monster. In all her anger the witch accidentally fell on top of the bush and landed in the thorns, which grabbed hold of her and squeezed her until she suffocated. At last the lovers realized they were truly free.

One afternoon, Rapunzel was very quiet and thoughtful. "You look sad, my dear Rapunzel," said the prince. "What's wrong?"

"I was thinking about my parents. For years I thought they were dead, but I know the witch lied to me. I have been wondering where they are and dreaming of seeing them, but I know this is impossible."

"Maybe it isn't! I will send knights to every corner of the kingdom. They will visit every village, town or city. I am sure that we will find them."

But the weeks passed, and there was no news. Finally, the day of the wedding came. Rapunzel felt so happy, but the day would not be perfect without her parents there. Suddenly the prince knocked on her door. "Rapunzel, I have a surprise!" he said.

"You cannot see the bride before the wedding. It's bad luck!" she said, laughing.

"In that case, I'll close my eyes, even if I will miss your smile."

Rapunzel opened the door and there were Nicolas and Anna, their eyes shining. She hugged them. Now her day was really perfect.

Hansel and Gretel

At the edge of the woods lived a woodcutter who was so poor, he barely had enough food for his wife and his two small children, Hansel and Gretel. As time went by things gradually got worse, until he was no longer able to provide for them.

One evening, when they were in the grip of hunger and despair the wife said to him: "Husband, we have no more food: tomorrow at dawn take the two children and give them each a small piece of bread, then take them into the woods with you, and when they are playing leave them there." Saddened and dismayed, the man exclaimed: "My wife, I don't have the courage to abandon my beloved children in the woods: the vicious beasts will surely kill them." His wife however was adamant: "If we keep going like this, we'll all starve to death," and she gave him no truce until the poor man gave in.

That evening the two children, who were hungry and unable to sleep, heard what the mother said to the father. Gretel became frightened and began to weep, but Hansel said: "Sister, don't worry, I've got an idea." Without making any noise the boy stood up, put on his jacket and slowly-slowly opened the door to go outside.

The moon was shining brightly on the white pebbles on the ground, which shimmered like brand new coins. Hansel picked up a big handful of pebbles, hid them inside his pockets and returned home. "Sleep easy, Gretel," he said and promptly fell asleep himself.

At the break of dawn, the mother woke them both: "Get up children, today we go into the woods. Here is a small piece of bread for each of you, but don't be greedy, save it until lunch."

Gretel put all the bread in her apron because Hansel's pockets were full of pebbles, then they walked into the woods. Along the way, Hansel let the pebbles he had collected the night before drop on the ground, one by one, without the parents noticing.

When they reached the depths of the woods, the father said: "Help gather some firewood to build a nice fire to keep us warm." Hansel and Gretel obeyed and when the fire was lit, the mother said: "Now lie next to the fire and rest; we are going to cut firewood. Wait here quietly, until we come back."

Hansel and Gretel remained beside the fire until noon, then they each ate a small piece of bread and trustingly waited until the evening for their parents to come back and get them.

By nightfall, Gretel became frightened and began to weep, but her brother said: "Don't despair, we just have to wait for the moon to rise."

When the moon rose into the dark sky, Hansel took Gretel by the hand: the pebbles shimmered under the light of the moon, showing them the way home. They walked all night and when they arrived home it was already morning. The father rejoiced to see his children safe and sound, but the mother was furious and pretended to be happy.

One evening after their return home, Hansel and Gretel heard the mother say to the father: "We have nothing to eat. Tomorrow you must lead the children in the deepest part of the woods so that they won't find their way back: there's no other way." The man felt his heart tighten with grief, but decided to follow his wife's demands.

Hearing the mother's words, Hansel got up to go collect more pebbles, but this time the door was locked. He returned to his bed, and to console Gretel he said: "Don't fret, sleep easy, the Lord will help us."

At daybreak the mother gave them each a small piece of bread. Along the path Hansel tore up the bread, dropping the crumbs on the ground to mark the way. The mother had brought them to a part of the woods where they had never been before. Like the previous time, the parents lit a fire and ordered the children to wait and keep warm, promising them to return before nightfall. At noon, Gretel shared her piece of bread with Hansel, who had used all of his along the way. At nightfall, no one came for them. Hansel consoled Gretel and said: "Wait for the moon to rise, so we'll be able to see the bread crumbs I scattered to find the way home." When the moon rose Hansel looked for the bread crumbs but found none: the forest birds had eaten them all!

Overcome by anguish, Hansel and Gretel walked all night and all of the following day, until they fell asleep exhausted.

When they awoke, they continued walking and searching for the way home, but instead they ventured deeper into the woods. They became tired, discouraged and hungry and, in the end, they drifted into a deep sleep.

On the third day, after having walked for many hours, they arrived at a strange little house made of candy and marzipan. It had transparent windows made of sugar: they couldn't believe their eyes!

The children were so hungry that in seeing all that goodness, they couldn't resist the temptation to dig in, but no sooner had Gretel started to gnaw at the door that a feeble voice came from inside: "Who's eating my candy house?"

The children did not answer and continued to eat. Suddenly the door opened and out came an old woman; Hansel and Gretel were so frightened that they dropped what they had in their hands.

Shaking her head, the old woman said: "How did you get here? Come on inside, you are welcome!" She took them by the hand and led them into the house where she cooked them a delicious dinner and prepared two beds with clean smelling sheets. Feeling safe, the children gratefully fell asleep.

In reality, the old woman was an evil witch who used her candy and marzipan house to attract children who were lost in the woods, and whenever she got her hands on one, she killed and cooked them, and ate them with great relish. That's why it's easy to understand why she was happy the two siblings had arrived at her house.

The following morning, before the kids woke up, the witch looked forward to a good feast and walked up to their beds to admire her prey.

Suddenly, before the poor boy could realize what was happening, she grabbed Hansel by the arm and locked him up inside a small cage.

Then she awoke Gretel with a jerk and said: "Go to the kitchen and prepare something good for your brother to eat, I want to fatten him up before I eat him!" Gretel had no choice but to do as she was told.

Every day Hansel was forced to eat huge amounts of food while Gretel almost starved. Every day the witch approached the cage and said: "Hansel, let me feel your finger, I want to see if you are fat enough." But Hansel, who had understood she had poor eyesight, instead of his finger poked out a small chicken bone he kept hidden. So the old witch thought he hadn't gained any weight. One evening a few weeks later, the witch said to Gretel: "Fat of skinny, tomorrow I will kill your brother and cook him. In the meantime, I am going to make some bread to bake in the oven; go fetch me some water." Feeling desperate, Gretel fetched the water in which the following day Hansel was supposed to cook.

The next morning, the little girl lit the fire and hung the pot full of water from a hook. While Gretel was in the kitchen, shaking with sobs, the witch called her and said gruffly: "Go and lean into the oven and tell me if the bread is baked: I can't see all the way to the back." Her real plan was to shove Gretel into the oven, let her roast, and then eat her in just a few bites. But Gretel, who had guessed the witch's intentions said: "I don't know how to look all the way to the back of the oven, show me first." And as soon as the witch leaned into the oven, Gretel gave her a big shove and quickly closed the door, securing it with an iron bolt. The witch began to scream, threatening her, then begging her, but Gretel ran off and left her to burn. She raced over to her brother and set him free.

The two children, embraced with great joy: at last, they could return to their parents!

The witch's house was filled with gold and gemstones: before setting off to find the way home, Hansel and Gretel took everything they could carry in their pockets and knapsacks. When they finally arrived, their father was overjoyed to see them again safe and sound. He'd been sad ever since abandoning his children, and the gold and gemstones that Hansel and Gretel brought home, allowed everyone to live without any more hardship.

Little Red Riding Hood

In a little cottage on the edge of the woods, there lived a little girl with her mother. She was loved by all for her cheerful, curious, sweet nature. The little girl, of course, had a name of her own, but because she always wore a red cloak with a hood, a present from her beloved grandmother, people had started calling her "Little Red Riding Hood," and the nickname pleased her so much that she adopted it. She was wearing her little red cloak when her mother gave her some bad news: "You grandmother will not be able to come to visit as she had promised you, my darling. Nothing serious has happened, but your grandmother has a bad cold so she has to stay in bed. She will not be able to get up for a few days: she has to rest!" "But how will she manage? Who will cook for her? Who will help her?" the little girl asked. "Let me go to her! I beg you, mama! I could stay with grandma for a few days and keep her company."

"I don't know: you'll have to go through the woods, you must be very careful…" said her mother anxiously. "I'll be careful! I promise!" said the girl.

"All right!" her mother said. "Take this basket with you, but please, follow the path!" Little Red Riding Hood promised her mother that she would be careful, then she took the basket with a fruit tart and left. Immediately she forgot all her mother's advice! The forest was looking so lovely that day: the birds were singing and the squirrels were jumping from one tree to another: they amused the girl so much that she started following them.

In no time at all Little Red Riding Hood found herself in the middle of the forest, the home of one of the most feared animals of the woods: the wolf.

The wolf could hear Little Red Riding Hood laughing from afar and decided to investigate.

He made his way through the bushes, saying to himself: "A little girl in the middle of the forest? She must have got lost, no one from the village ever comes here. Bad for her and good for me: I am about to have a delicious little meal!" And as he said this, he came out of his hiding place, walked towards her and asked her with a sinister smile: "Hello, little girl, what is your name? And what are you doing in this part of the forest?"

"I am Little Red Riding Hood, I am going to visit my grandmother who is ill." On hearing her reply, the wolf began toying with the idea of gobbling up both Little Red Riding Hood and the grandmother, but to do this he would have to get to the grandmother's house before Little Red Riding Hood! There he would attack the grandmother and then wait for the granddaughter to arrive.

But first he had to get rid of the girl for long enough to reach the grandmother's house. The wolf flashed his long, sharp teeth beneath his whiskers, then asked the girl: "Wouldn't you like to take her flowers too? There are very pretty flowers not far from here," the wolf lied. "I love flowers! They would be perfect to cheer up my grandmother," Little Red Riding Hood replied excitedly, "Wolf, please tell me where I can find them."

"Continue along that path until you get to a waterfall," the wolf explained, telling the girl a much longer way along the main road so as to give himself enough time to reach the grandmother's house before her. "Thank you! You are much kinder than people say!" Little Red Riding Hood replied, as she set off in the direction indicated by the animal.

"Good girl, go into the forest while I run to your grandmother's house!" the wolf thought to himself, watching the girl until she disappeared behind a big oak tree.

When he was sure that Little Red Riding Hood would not be turning back, the wolf leapt for joy, then he made his way in the opposite direction and ran through the forest to the grandmother's house, arriving there well before Little Red Riding Hood! The wolf laughed: he had made it in time for his plan to succeed.

He knocked at the door, cleared his throat and then, imitating the little girl's voice, he said: "It's me, grandma, Little Red Riding Hood."

"Little one, you have come to visit me? Come in, my dear, the door is open."

And the wolf went in, leapt on the bed and gobbled up the grandmother in a single mouthful. Then he lay down in the grandmother's bed, having put on her clothes, her bonnet and her glasses.

As he had expected, Little Red Riding Hood soon arrived. When she knocked on the door, the wolf imitated the grandmother's voice, asking: "Who is it?"

"It's me, Little Red Riding Hood," the girl replied. "What a lovely surprise, my dear, do come in and say hello to your grandmother!" The little girl pushed the door open, walked to the bed and said: "Grandma, you look strange to me! What big eyes you have!"

"All the better to see you with, my dear," the wolf replied.

"And what big ears you have!"

"All the better to hear you with."

"And what a big mouth you have!"

"All the better to eat you with!" the wolf shouted, leaping on the little girl. And in no time at all no trace remained of Little Red Riding Hood.

Some say that this was the end of the story: the wolf, feeling full, left the cottage and walked contentedly into the thick of the forest. But others say that, while the wolf was snoring in the grandmother's bed, a hunter passing by the cottage heard the noise and went in. He saw the wolf fast asleep with his belly bloated. So he took out his knife and was about to attack when the animal's belly suddenly moved. He cut open the wolf's stomach and, to his surprise, Little Red Riding Hood and her grandmother jumped out, terrified and in a sorry state but safe and sound! They embraced each other, then thanked the hunter sincerely: "I had given up all hope of anyone being able to save us!" the grandmother said, deeply moved. "I had been trying to catch this wolf for a long time," the hunter replied. "Today is a very special day for me. Now I can go home." In saying so, the hunter hoisted the heavy corpse of the wolf onto his shoulders and walked slowly home, leaving Little Red Riding Hood and her grandmother to celebrate with a slice of fruit tart and plenty of cuddles.

Puss in Boots

Once upon a time there was an old miller who owned nothing apart other than mill, a donkey and a cat. When he was approaching the end of his days, the division of his possessions between his three sons was therefore quickly done: he left his mill to the first and his donkey to the second. "And to you," he said to the youngest son, "I cannot leave you anything but the cat."

Having been left on his own, the young lad had a look at the animal: "I know you are a good cat and I love you," he said, scratching his head. "But if you are really as cunning as they say, quickly go and leave me alone with my misery. With what I possess, I can only promise you three things: cold in the winter, warmth in the summer and hunger all the year round."

Until then the cat, like every other cat, had never spoken a word, but now it winked and suddenly began to speak: "My boy, you must do just two things, find me a pair of boots and trust my intelligence. Away with hunger: within three months we will be at court!" Once he had overcome his amazement the young lad, though not believing these words, decided to pander to the cat's eccentric plan, so he found two little worn-out boots and gave them to the creature. With a couple of bounds the cat ran off into the wood, swiftly went to work and, great hunter that he was, in less than an hour he had captured a beautiful rabbit. Satisfied, he went to court and asked to be received by the king. Paying great respect to the king, the cat said: "Sire, pray accept this rabbit that my owner, your loyal servant the Marquis of Carabas, has sent to you."

"Tell your master that I thank him and that I am very grateful for his gift; it is really good of him to give what he has caught to the table of His Majesty," replied the king, deeply moved by this completely unexpected generosity.

The following morning the cat went to hide in the middle of a field of wheat and caught two partridges, then he went to the king again.

"Sire," he said, "I am bringing you another modest tribute from my lord and master, the Marquis of Carabas."

That evening the king, curious about the source of the two gifts, consulted the Almanac of the Nobility where he looked in a vain for this unknown marquis, while his daughter, the beautiful princess, began to dream of possibly marrying with this man who was so generous and considerate.

In short, every morning for more than a month, the clever cat presented himself at court with mouth-watering gifts from the Marquis of Carabas, his lord and master. Then one day he achieved his aim and, chatting with the king whose trust he now enjoyed, he discovered that on the following day the princess would be taking a long carriage ride along the river bank.

The cat ran to bring the news to the young man saying: "If you follow my instructions, your fortune will be made! Listen carefully: tomorrow morning you are going to bathe in the river, at the place I will tell you, and when the king's carriage appears, do not contradict anything I say; just leave everything to me."

The next day the cat hid behind a bush on the side of the road and, when he saw the royal carriage arriving, he burst out of his hiding place, moved to the middle of the road and began to shout, waving his arms and asking for help: "Your Majesty, I beg you to help me!" the cat shouted when the carriage had stopped and the king had got out to see what was going on. "Please help my master, the Marquis of Carabas! Some evil people have robbed him, then stolen his fine clothes and thrown him into the river to drown."

Without hesitation, the king ordered the pages, cupbearers, chamberlains and counselors, who were part of his large entourage, to go and help his most generous and noble subject, while two couriers on horseback immediately went back to the castle to collect the most sumptuous robes that they could find inside the royal wardrobe.

The young man was fished out of the river and offered a ride to the castle in the royal carriage. An encouraging look from the cat convinced him to accept the invitation and, without having any idea of the animal's plan, to climb into the carriage.

When the princess saw the mysterious marquis she was much impressed and the young man was also enchanted by her beauty. Happy to see that everything was going according to plan, the cat put the second part of his scheme into effect: running by leaps and bounds ahead of the carriage, he stopped only when, along the road, he met some peasants setting off to harvest the corn. "Good people," he said, "I don't have time to explain, but be aware that if you don't tell everyone that these fields belong to the Marquis of Carabas, you will end up cut into little pieces for meat balls."

So when the king's carriage reached them and the king asked the peasants who was the lord of these lands, they immediately replied: "They belong to the Marquis of Carabas."

The cat, still running ahead of the carriage, repeated the same thing to anyone he met along the road.

The king never stopped being amazed at the great wealth of the Marquis of Carabas. Finally, the cat arrived at a beautiful castle where a terrible ogre lived, and who was the real owner of the lands that the carriage had traveled through. When the cat reached the drawbridge the terrifying

voice of the ogre greeted him. "Who are you? How dare you enter my castle? You will pay with your life!"

The cat was not intimidated and in a challenging manner he declared: "You say you are a great magician. I have been told that you have the ability to change your appearance and turn yourself into any animal, that with the greatest of ease you could become a lion or an elephant. Other people say that's a lie…"

"It is true," the ogre replied abruptly, "and to prove it I will become a lion in front of your very eyes." In a flash, in place of the ogre there was an enormous lion that with a powerful roar made the cat leap onto the roof. "Really impressive!" said the cat when it had come down. "In fact I can see it is quite easy for you to turn yourself into such a large beast. But I think it would be impossible for you to become a very much smaller animal, for example a mouse…"

"Impossible?" said the ogre, "Wait and see!" In saying so, he changed into a mouse and began running around the floor. The cat, who was expecting this, leapt upon the mouse in a flash and… devoured it in one gulp.

At that moment the king's carriage arrived at the castle and the cat came down into the courtyard to greet him. "Your Majesty, welcome to the palace of the Marquis of Carabas!" he exclaimed. The king was amazed by the castle's elegance and riches, and having been won over by the character of the young man whom his daughter now loved, he gladly agreed to their wedding.

So it was that the miller's son married princess, but, since he was honest and sincere, he did not want to continue the deception.

He told her what had really happened, explaining every detail of what the cat had contrived, from the first lucky hunt in the forest to the master stroke of killing the ogre and taking the castle. Freed from guilt by this confession, he passed many happy years with his wife. And the cat? He took off his boots and from that day on he lived at the castle, where he spent the days curled up on soft cushions, enjoying delicious bowls of cream.

Tom Thumb

At the edge of the great forest there was a little house, small and modest, in which there lived a family consisting of a woodcutter, his wife, and seven children, all boys. The youngest of these, a clever, lively child seven years old, was considered very special by everyone, because when he came into the world, he was not much bigger than a thumb, and even growing up he remained tiny, which is why everyone called him Tom Thumb.

The family lived in poverty, but the woodcutter always managed to provide a hot meal for his loved ones. But then there was a tragic year in which the famine was so bad that there was nothing to eat for days on end. One evening, having put the children to bed, with a breaking heart he woodcutter said to his wife, "As you can see, we cannot feed our family: if the children stay with us they will end up dying of hunger and I could not bear it, so I have decided to take them into the woods."

"You are going to leave them in the woods? And how will they survive? If we abandon them they will die!" said the distraught woman. He replied: "It's the only way: without those mouths to feed, in a few days we can save the money needed to survive the winter, then we will go back and get them." The mother ended up accepting the situation and went to bed crying, not realizing that Tom Thumb, hidden behind the chair, had heard them talking, and he had started thinking about a solution. When he was sure that everyone was asleep, he went outside and walked along a river bank where he filled his pockets with white pebbles, then, without being heard, he went back to bed.

The next day the father took the boys into the woods with him. When they had reached the depths of the forest, the woodcutter went to work, while the boys played at making bows and arrows. Seeing that they were distracted, their father slowly walked away and disappeared into the trees. When the brothers realized that they were alone, they began to cry and scream loudly, all but Tom Thumb. He knew he could find his way home because, in the morning, he had dropped the white pebbles that he had hidden in his pocket along the path. Following them back, the children returned home and there they found their father and mother crying, saying: "Where are the children now? Our poor children?" The brothers,

who were hidden behind the door, heard them and all together shouted: "We are here! We are here!" The mother immediately ran to open the door and, embracing them, let them in.

As luck would have it, the next day the debtors paid the money they owed the father and for a few weeks the family could live without worrying. But when all the money had been spent, they began to suffer from hunger again, so the parents decided to take the children into the woods. Again, Tom Thumb heard everything and he thought he would go outside for pebbles as he had before, but every night he found the door barred so he could not go out. In the morning when they walked into the woods, Tom Thumb took the loaf of bread that his mother had given him for breakfast, and which instead of eating he broke into little pieces.

When he was in the cart with the other brothers, he scattered the crumbs along the road leading into the forest without being noticed. In the evening when the parents left the children in a clearing, far away from home, the brothers did not despair because they knew that Tom Thumb would easily find the way home by following the crumbs scattered along the path. But to their disappointment they saw that the crumbs were gone: the birds had eaten them all! Tom Thumb did not lose heart and climbed to the top of a tree to see if he could see his parents' house in the distance. Looking in all directions, eventually he saw a little light: it could not be their home, but it would be a safe shelter for keeping warm. He climbed down the tree and explained his plan to the brothers, then he led them to that part of the forest. They arrived at a house and knocked on the door. A pleasant-looking woman opened it and asked what they wanted. Tom Thumb said that they had were lost in the forest and asked if they could stay for the night, but the woman said: "Dear me! Don't you know that this is the home of the ogre who eats little children?" The brothers began to tremble and cry, until the ogre's wife, certain that her husband would not return until the morning, let them in and hid them in a small room upstairs, where the children found seven little beds in which they lay down, cold and exhausted.

Just then, however, they heard a frightening noise downstairs, three blows that almost broke the door down: the ogre was back home already. The huge monster, with merciless eyes and an enormous mouth, carried a whole wild boar on his back, which he dropped to the ground at his wife's the feet. He took off his boots and then, sniffing the air, he roared: "Hey, hey, I smell little children! Who have you let in, woman?" he asked his wife angrily.

"No one! You are mistaken! What you are smelling is the roast meat that is cooking for you on the fire. And I could also cook this boar now, if you like." The ogre was so hungry that he decided to have dinner at once: he would find out later if someone was hiding in his house, and it would be so much the worse for them! But during dinner his wife, knowing how much he liked wine, gave him so much that the ogre collapsed asleep in front of the fire. The children were sleeping too, all but Tom Thumb. When he saw from the top of the stairs that the way was clear, he woke up the brothers and told them to get dressed immediately and to tie all the sheets together. Then, one by one, they lowered themselves from the window, but at that moment the ogre woke up and looked out, just in time to see the last child climbing over the garden wall to escape into the woods. Angrily shouting to his wife to bring him his magic boots, in which he could run as fast as the wind, he went in pursuit of the children. They continued running but behind them the ogre was approaching by leaps and bounds. His boots enabled him to climb over tree trunks and giant boulders and to jump over rivers as if they were streams. Tom Thumb hid the brothers behind a rock, then waited for the ogre. When the monster arrived, he sat down to rest on the very same rock that was concealing the children, then with a groan he took off the boots that were also very uncomfortable. Tom Thumb slowly approached, grabbed the discarded boots, and put them on. Then he jumped out of hiding and challenged the ogre to catch him as he ran away, quick as a flash. The ogre pursued him furiously for over an hour, but when Tom Thumb jumped over a chasm in one leap, the ogre fell right into it.

The child then went back to the ogre's house and reassured the kind woman: the monster would never come back! Beside herself with joy, the woman gave the child all the ogre's riches to thank him for putting an end to her imprisonment. So Tom Thumb and his brothers went back to their parents' house bringing with them treasure chests filled with gold and precious stones, and the family never knew poverty again.

Cinderella

A rich merchant, recently widowed, took a difficult decision so as not to leave his young daughter alone during his long business journeys. Before setting off again he would re-marry so as to give the little girl a mother, even though he knew that no one could ever replace his wife in both their hearts.

His new wife already had two daughters and the widower hoped that the stepsisters would be pleasant playmates for his little girl, keeping her company and helping her bear her father's absence and the loss of her mother more easily.

So he set off on a long journey, without realizing that the stepmother would soon reveal herself to be a selfish, overbearing woman, and that the two stepsisters, vain and cruel like their mother, would make his little daughter's life very hard and sad. She was given the lowliest chores in the house: she had to do the dishes, clean the stairs and sweep her stepsisters' beautiful bedrooms; and when she had finished her work, there would be a biscuit, always covered in cinders, waiting for her near the fireplace. This was why her two sisters had given her the unkind nickname of Cinderella.

Long years passed in this way, without anything changing in Cinderella's life, but she never lost her sweet, kind nature. At last the moment came when things began to change: one day an invitation arrived for a great court ball, during which, it was said, the prince would choose his future wife.

The stepsisters, happy and excited, spent days choosing the dresses and hairstyles that would suit them best, so that Cinderella had to iron heaps of linen and starch yards of brocade and lace.

At home all the talk was about the ball: "I," said the elder stepsister, "I shall wear the red velvet gown trimmed with English lace."

"And I," said the younger one, "shall wear my velvet gown with the mantle of gold flowers and a diamond necklace, so I shall be sure not go unnoticed." The day of the ball finally arrived and the stepsisters put on their clothes, then they called Cinderella to give her opinion, knowing that she had good taste. The young girl did her best to advise them and offered to do their hair. Then, as she helped them dress, the stepsisters asked her: "Would you like to go to the ball?"

"Oh, yes! It would be a dream come true!" she replied, hoping for an invitation. "More like a nightmare! Look at yourself: do you think you can go to court with those clothes, covered in cinders?" the sisters laughed cruelly.

When the carriage left, taking the sisters to the castle, Cinderella watched it as long as she could, then when she no longer saw it, she began to cry. At that moment, a lady came up to her and asked what had happened. "Well, I would like…" but she was sobbing so hard that she was unable to speak. The lady, who was in fact a fairy, said to her: "I would like to see you happy tonight. So tell me: what would you like? To go to the ball?" "Yes, but I cannot: I am wearing rags and I do not know how to get to the castle, and also, what would I do if my stepmother recognized me?"

"No one will recognize you, little girl: foolish people usually judge by appearances, unfortunately, and your stepmother is no exception. Looking at the lady you will have become, she will only see a young noblewoman; she will not be able to see any similarity to the stepdaughter she left at home cleaning the house. Now I shall get to work. Fetch me a pumpkin."

"I shall go and get one from the vegetable garden," said Cinderella, confused. She did not see how a pumpkin could help her to go to the ball, but the lady was the first person to offer to help her for a long time and she did not want to stand in her way. She took the largest pumpkin she could find in the garden and brought it to the fairy who, raising her hands, whispered a few words that Cinderella could not make out. At once the pumpkin began to grow and transform itself, until it had become an elegant carriage. At the sight of it Cinderella was speechless, but the fairy's magic had only just started!

A lizard sleeping on a branch became a liveried coachman and two little mice peeping out of their nest were transformed into white horses.

"It is done! So, Cinderella, are you ready?" asked the fairy, satisfied with her work. "I… yes, thank you so much, I cannot wait to go to the ball! But shall I wear these tattered old clothes?" Cinderella asked. "Oh, what a scatterbrain I am, my dear! No, absolutely not!" And in saying so, she gathered a handful of almond petals and threw them in the air.

As soon as she said the magic words, the almond petals turned into the most elegant gown the girl had ever seen. The fairy inspected her and with a critical look she said "Only the shoes are missing!" Then with a word she made two dainty shoes appear on Cinderella's feet: they were crystal and sparkled like diamonds. "Now you really look like a princess. But there is one condition: you must be home before the clock strikes midnight. Don't be late! And now go and have fun, my little one."

When Cinderella made her entrance, the whole ballroom fell silent: no one had ever seen a young girl so beautiful and with such a regal air. All the noblewomen in the ballroom immediately realized that they could never compete with her smile or her sparkling eyes.

Cinderella was the picture of happiness and the prince immediately realized that he wanted no one but her at his side that evening, so he approached and, with a bow, presented himself and asked her to dance. He then took her by the hand and danced all night with her: he did not want to dance with anyone else. Cinderella felt she was living a dream but when she heard the clock start striking midnight, she remembered the fairy's words and, whispering her excuses, she freed her hand from the prince's, rushed through the palace and ran down the stairs.

She lost one of her glass shoes but she did not stop, for fear that the prince would catch up with her.

Indeed, the prince had followed her down the staircase, determined to stop the mysterious young girl if only to discover her name, but he was only in time to see her climb into a sumptuous carriage and disappear into the night. Devastated, he suddenly saw the shoe that she had lost and picked it up with great care. When the two stepsisters returned from the ball, Cinderella asked them if they had had fun. Annoyed, the girls told her about the mysterious lady who had run away as midnight struck, who had been in such

a rush that she had lost one of her glass shoes. The king's son had found it and picked it up and he had spent the rest of the ball gazing at it: naturally they were furious, assuming that he must have fallen madly in love with the beautiful girl who had lost her shoe. And they were right, as they discovered a few days later when the king's son asked the heralds to proclaim that he would marry only the girl whose foot fitted this shoe. He began by asking all the duchesses to try it on, then all the ladies of the court, but in vain.

The two stepsisters were also asked to try on the shoe. Each did her best to force her foot into it, but in vain. "Have you any other daughters, madam?" the page asked their mother. "No!" she replied. "Then who is that young girl?" he asked, pointing at Cinderella who was looking at her shoe in amazement from the top of the stairs. "She is only the maid!" the exasperated stepmother replied. "I have orders to try the shoe on every young girl in the kingdom," the royal servant said firmly. Cinderella approached and, ignoring the smirks of her sisters, slipped her foot into the shoe without any difficulty. The two sisters were astonished and the stepmother suddenly recognized her as the beautiful lady she had seen at the ball. Without a moment's hesitation they threw themselves at her feet and asked her forgiveness for all the ill-treatment they had inflicted on her. Cinderella told them to get up and embraced them, saying that she forgave them with all her heart; then she followed the page to the carriage that would take her to the royal palace where she could at last tell the prince her name and explain to him everything that had happened.

A month later a magnificent party took place during which Cinderella married the prince and all the bells in the kingdom rang to celebrate the joyous event.

And from that day on the two young people lived happily ever after.

The Brementown Musicians

A man owned a donkey that had faithfully served him for many years, without ever giving in to exhaustion, but was now old and lacking in strength and unable to work as hard. The master decided to put him down, but the donkey, having realized his predicament, decided to escape. He headed toward the city of Bremen, where he hoped to join the town band.

After walking awhile, the donkey met a hunting dog that was lying on the side of the road and breathing heavily from running.

"Why are you panting so hard?" asked the donkey.

"Oh…" replied the dog, "Now that I am old and too weak to keep hunting, my master was going to get rid of me, so I fled as fast as I could, but now I wonder how I am going to make a living and survive."

"I am going to Bremen to join the town band, come with me" said the donkey. The dog accepted his invitation and together they resumed he journey.

After a short time, they met a cat that looked very sad.

"What happened to you?" asked the donkey.

"I am getting older and my teeth are not as sharp as they used to be, instead of hunting mice, I'd rather keep warm next to the stove. So my mistress tried to drown me, but I managed to escape and now I don't know where to go or what to do."

"Come to Bremen with us and we'll all join the town band." The cat agreed and went with the donkey and the dog.

Along the way, the threesome passed a courtyard with a henhouse, inside which a rooster was making a lot of noise.

"Why are you squawking so loud?" asked the donkey.

"Tomorrow is a holiday and the mistress has invited her relatives to dinner; she ordered the cook to wring my neck because she wants me as the main course," the rooster answered between one shriek and the next.

"Stop crying," said the donkey. "Come to Bremen with us: you have a loud voice and together we'll perform a beautiful concert!"

The rooster accepted the offer and the four new friends resumed the journey.

At nightfall the group stopped in the woods to rest. The donkey and the dog lay under a tree, while the cat and the rooster looked for a safe spot high up in the branches. Before going to sleep, the rooster took a look around and noticed a tiny light shining in the distance: surely it was a house. Excited, he flew over to tell his comrades, and together they decided to get back on the road to reach the clearing where the light was coming form. At last they arrived at the house, which was all lit and occupied by a gang of robbers. The donkey, which was the tallest, walked up to the window and looked inside. "What do you see?" asked the rooster impatiently.

"I see a table surrounded by a bunch of robbers enjoying a nice feast," replied the donkey.

"It would be nice if it were us instead of the robbers," sighed the rooster.

The four animals decided to come up with a plan to scare the robbers away. The donkey leaned his forefeet against the windowsill, the dog jumped on the donkey's back, the cat jumped on top of the dog, and the rooster flew on top of the cat's head. In this fashion, they began their concert: the donkey brayed as loudly as he could, the dog barked incessantly, the cat meowed, and the rooster crowed at the top of his voice. They made a terrible din! At that moment, the donkey gave a signal and the four animals burst through the window, shattering the glass and terrorizing the robbers, who all fled into the woods. Overjoyed, the four friends sat at the table and ate until they almost burst, then they went to sleep, each choosing a spot that was most suited to their habits. The donkey found a comfortable bed in the dunghill, the dog settled behind the door, the cat slept next to the fireplace, and the rooster flew up to a beam. They all fell into a deep sleep.

Meanwhile the robbers, who were hiding in the depth of the woods, tried to understand what happened and what caused them to be so frightened to flee without even looking back. The captain decided to send one of his men to investigate the situation. The robber cautiously approached the house and took a look inside, trying to see the enemy in the darkness.

Everything appeared calm, there was no suspicious noise and the house looked more or less how they'd left it, except for the table, on which there were only a few leftovers. The robber decided to get some light so he could take a closer look: next to the fireplace he saw two glowing embers, which he approached to light a matchstick. But those embers were none other than the glowing eyes of the cat, who leaped at him, scratching him in the face. The terrified robber tried to escape through the door, but he stumbled over the dog, who promptly bit him in the leg. The poor robber ran into the court-yard where he passed the donkey, who had been awoken by all the commo-tion and kicked him hard in the behind. Meanwhile, the rooster crowed vic-toriously from a high beam. Seized by terror, the robber fled, running as fast as he could until he reached his companions. In a whimper he said: "There's a horrible and cruel witch in the house, she assaulted me and scratched my face with nails as sharp as blades; guarding the door is an armed man who stabbed me with a knife and inflicted a deep wound in my leg; in the court-yard near the dunghill, there's a monster that struck me with a heavy club, and finally, on the roof there's a judge who in a horrendous voice cries: 'chain that robber!' It's a miracle I managed to escape!"

From that day onward the robbers decided to stay away from the house and the four Bremen town musicians were so comfortable there that they decided to stay and to end their journey.

Snow White

During a cold winter morning, the queen sat by the window. For some time, she and her husband, the king, desired to become parents; how wonderful their life would be with a child! While lost in thought, she accidentally pricked her finger and a drop of blood trickled out. As she watched this, she thought, "I wish for a charming and cheerful child, with lips as red as this drop of blood, hair as black as coal, and skin as white as snow." A good fairy must have heard the queen's prayer, because soon after, her wish came true. When the child was born, she was named Snow White. But soon, the queen was struck by an unknown illness, which none of the doctors summoned from all over the kingdom were able to cure.

For months after the queen's death, the king spent all his time comforting his daughter.

But as he had many duties, the kingdom needed him to rule. He decided to marry again. When the new bride's carriage arrived at court one cold autumn morning, the crowd that gathered to see her was enchanted. She curtsied before the king, who greeted her, then entered the castle followed by two footmen who carefully carried a large, heavy parcel shrouded in cloth. When she was alone in her room, the queen approached the parcel and, throwing the cloth aside, revealed a mirror that she propped up against the wall. No one suspected that in reality, she was a powerful witch. The mirror, which she took with her everywhere, was magic. Looking at it she said, "Mirror, mirror on the wall, who is the fairest of them all?"

At that, the mirror came alive. From within golden sparks arose, which began to swirl and finally took the shape of a face that replied, "My queen, in all the kingdom, there is none more beautiful than you."

Every evening, the queen looked in the mirror, and every time she asked the same question and heard the same answer.

As the years passed, Snow White grew increasingly like her mother from whom she had inherited kindness, gaiety and beauty.

One day, hearing Snow White's laughter, the stepmother went out on the terrace, suddenly she noticed that Snow White had become a beautiful young woman.

"Surely, no woman in the world is more beautiful than me!" The queen hurried back to her chambers and, as she uncovered the mirror, she thought there was only one way to be sure.

"Mirror, mirror on the wall, who is the fairest of them all?" she asked.

"You will not be happy with what I have to say. Your Majesty, you are beautiful, but Snow White is more beautiful than you," the mirror replied.

When she heard these words, the queen became incensed. The next day, she summoned the royal huntsman. When the man arrived she said, "Huntsman, I have a special task for you that must remain between us."

"My queen, I will do anything you ask!" he said.

"You must kill Snow White!" whispered the queen. "Take her into the woods, today. When you return, say there was a tragic accident and she died. Bring me her heart in this!" She gave the huntsman's a bejeweled box.

Snow White loved the woods and was glad the huntsman suggested a walk. The huntsman, however, held his head low. He knew if he didn't kill Snow White, the queen would not spare his life. When Snow White's back was turned, he pulled out his knife and slowly approached her intending to kill her. Yet, at the last moment, he cried, "I can't! My child, I cannot harm you!"

Snow White saw the knife in the huntsman's hand and the tears streaming down his cheeks. The man fell to his knees and confessed everything.

"My stepmother? I... I don't believe it!" Snow White exclaimed.

"You must, my child. This woman is evil and will stop at nothing to destroy you!" The huntsman said.

"But where shall I go?" Snow White was weeping.

"It doesn't matter child! Go now! Run! RUN!" the huntsman cried.

Snow White embraced him then fled.

The huntsman watched her and then he walked further into the woods. He found a wild boar and killed it with his bow. He put its heart into the bejeweled box, then returned to the castle where the queen waited impatiently. "Well?" she asked when he arrived at her quarters. "Have you done what I ordered?"

"Yes, Your Majesty. You no longer need to worry about Snow White," he said, giving her the box. When she opened it, she began to laugh uncontrollably.

Meanwhile Snow White was terrified. She had never been in the woods at night.

In the darkness, the trees that she climbed during

the day seemed scary, their branches looked like monstrous arms wanting to grab her.

She ran for hours, without knowing where she was going. At last, she caught sight of a cottage at the center of a clearing. Through a window, she saw the glowing light of an open fire. Snow White stood at the door and knocked timidly. There was no reply. Snow White knocked harder and the door opened slightly. There was no one home. "I could wait by the fire until the owner comes back."

Snow White looked around and was surprised that everything in the room was pint-sized. The table was set with seven little plates, and on the dresser she saw that there were such tiny cups. By the fire there was a chair like the one she had as a child. In the corner of the room there was a staircase, which she decided to climb. She found seven tiny beds. She was so tired that she lay down on one and fell fast asleep. Soon after, the cottage's inhabitants returned. They were seven dwarfs who certainly didn't expect to find a beautiful girl fast asleep in one of their beds.

"She is beautiful!" whispered the youngest. "Shh! Don't shout! You'll wake her!" said the wisest.

"I am already awake," said Snow White, opening her eyes.

"I'm Snow White and I am sorry to have come into your house without permission, but I didn't know where else to go. I no longer have a home," said Snow White, her eyes bright with tears.

"In that case you must stay!" the youngest dwarf said.

Meanwhile, the stepmother was in her room standing before the mirror. When she asked who the most beautiful woman was, the mirror replied, "You are the most beautiful within the castle walls, but Snow White is still alive, and she is more beautiful than you."

"What? But that's impossible!" cried the queen. "Prove that she is still alive!"

Snow White's face appeared in the mirror. She was laughing and surrounded by the seven dwarfs. In seeing this, the queen became pale. "The huntsman lied to me," she hissed. "I will have to go to Snow White myself."

In a flash, the queen left the room and ran down the castle stairs into the cellar where she kept books on black magic hidden.

She grabbed a huge pot underneath which she lit a greenish fire. One by one, she added the ingredients to the cauldron, concocting a ghastly mixture. When it was ready, she dipped an apple into the fuming brew. Pleased, she then prepared a magic potion that she drank to transform herself into a grinning old fruit seller.

And so she set out into the woods. Meanwhile, in the cottage, Snow White was unaware of having been discovered by the stepmother and, without suspecting her evil plans, she was enjoying herself: dancing, singing and playing music with her new friends!

The next morning, while the dwarfs were at work mining for gemstones, Snow White cleaned the house, washed the laundry, then decided to bake a lovely cake.

At that same moment, she heard a voice calling, "Apples! Red, juicy apples!"

It was an old woman, carrying a basket filled with the most beautiful apples Snow White had ever seen.

"Just in time!"

"It's your lucky day, my dear. These apples will make a delicious pie," the queen said. "Here, try one."

She offered Snow White the reddest and shiniest apple in the basket, and as soon as Snow White bit into it, her head began to swim. She then fell to the floor and everything went black. When the dwarves returned home, they found Snow White lying on the ground next to the bitten apple. After trying desperately to revive her, they realized there was nothing they could do to awaken the girl form a sleep that seemed as deep as death itself. The seven dwarfs decided they would lay their friend in an open crystal coffin in the middle of the clearing. They spent days carving the rock. When it was ready, they placed Snow White inside and decorated it with flowers.

The summer passed and autumn arrived, but Snow White did not awaken. After many months of grief, the dwarfs knew she never would.

One day, when they came home from work, they saw a young nobleman standing beside the crystal coffin. He was riding past the clearing when he saw Snow White lying there.

"Stop! Don't you dare touch her!" the dwarfs shouted, grasping their axes.

"I mean her no harm, I assure you," said the prince without taking his eyes off the beautiful girl. "Is she asleep?" the prince asked.

"She has fallen under an evil spell," explained the dwarfs. "She has been asleep for months and there is no way of waking her."

The prince approached Snow White and delicately kissed her smiling lips.

To the dwarfs' astonishment, Snow White stirred. Her smile widened and then her eyelids fluttered open, at last she turned and looked at the prince.

The prince took her hand and asked her to follow him to his castle and become his bride. Snow White smiled and said, "I will, because I love you more than any other."

Snow White and the prince married as soon as they arrived at his castle.

Charles Perrault

French storyteller Charles Perrault published his "Tales of Mother Goose" in 1697; the first — and most important, at least up till that moment — collection of fairy tales based on popular and rural story-telling traditions, both prose and poetry. The book, which met with instant success, definitely contributed to spreading its characters' adventures throughout Europe.

At the time, Perrault could have no idea that some of his tales would still be familiar to and loved by children all over the world, over four hundred years later!

Sleeping Beauty, for example, is one of his best-known tales, but not everyone knows them all…

Turn the pages and see if you can find any fairy tales you'd never heard of before…

Ricky with the Tuft

Once upon a time there were a king and a queen who were longing for a baby. You can imagine their joy when they realized that their wish had finally come true. And yet, when the baby was born, both found it difficult to hide their concern about the baby's appearance: he was the ugliest baby they had ever seen! He was cross-eyed, his nose was squashed, and his ears were large and stuck out, but the queen loved him immediately. The only thing she disliked was the weird tuft of hair that invariably remained sticking up however hard she tried to brush it. Soon this tuft earned Prince Ricky the affectionate nickname of "Ricky with the Tuft" among his subjects. A powerful fairy was invited to the baby's christening and she gave him an exceptional gift that endowed the baby not only with intelligence and wit, but also with the power of giving wisdom to the person he loved. And the fairy godmother's spell came true: as soon as the baby started talking, it immediately became obvious that he was extremely intelligent and amusing, a quality that made him much loved throughout the kingdom.

As it happened, in the meantime the queen of a neighboring country had given birth to two little daughters. The first was the most beautiful young girl, but the other was so ugly that her appearance scared people. The queen was very concerned and invited the same fairy who had attended Ricky's christening to her court so that she could use her benevolent powers on the two little princesses as well: "Don't despair, Your Highness," said the fairy, foretelling the babies' future very clearly. "The little girl who has not been rewarded with good looks will be so intelligent that whoever gets to know her will no longer notice her lack of beauty."

"Let us hope so," the queen replied. "But would it not be possible to do same thing for the other little girl, who is so stunningly beautiful?"

"So far as that is concerned, I can do nothing, my lady," the fairy replied. "Your second daughter will become an enchanting young woman but an extremely stupid one. However I shall grant her one gift: she will have the power to make the person she loves beautiful."

The years passed and, at the same time as the princesses grew, so did their gifts, so much so that people spoke of nothing else but the beauty of the elder one and the intelligence of the younger one. But as the years went by their

faults also became increasingly pronounced. The younger daughter became more and more ugly while the older one became the most beautiful young girl in the entire kingdom! And yet she was not the one who drew people's attention: when they were together in public, people would first flock round the beautiful one so as to see and admire her, but very soon they realized that she had nothing interesting to say and preferred instead to go and listen to the younger sister.

The beautiful sister, although she was indeed very stupid, suffered very much from this situation and one day, no longer able to bear the humiliation of looking foolish all the time, she ran away crying in the park. It was then that she saw coming towards her a creature who had a horrifying appearance but was dressed with amazing elegance. It was Ricky with the Tuft who had fallen in love with the princess after seeing her portrait, and he had traveled for days to see her. When the prince saw her tears, he asked: "How is it that a beautiful girl like you could be so sad? Beauty is such a great gift that nothing should ever hurt anyone who is endowed with it."

The princess replied: "Believe me, I would much rather be ugly but intelligent like my sister, rather than beautiful and stupid."

"If that is what makes you so unhappy, then I can help you."

"How?" asked the princess.

"At my birth I received a magic gift: I have the power to give the person I choose as my companion all the intelligence she wants. I love you very much, Your Highness, and if you promise to marry me I shall be happy to give you what you so much long to have." The princess looked at him as she tried to decide what the best choice would be, but all this thinking gave her an incredible headache, so she pulled a face that her admirer misunderstood.

"I understand why you are hesitating, I am well aware of my appearance, but I have no intention of giving up. This is what we shall do: if you agree to give me your hand in marriage, you will have a whole year, starting from today, to change your mind, but in the meantime, you will allow me from now on to share with you all my intelligence as a wedding gift. What do you say?" Without thinking of the consequences, the princess immediately accepted Ricky's proposal: she would marry him a year from now, on the same day. As soon as she had made this promise, she suddenly felt different; she delt she could see everything that surrounding her with greater clarity, and from that moment on she always showed remarkable intelligence and wisdom.

When she returned to the palace, no one knew what to think of this incredibly sudden and unexpected change, news of which soon became known far beyond the confines of the kingdom. The young princes in neighboring countries suddenly competed to win her hand, but none of them managed to win the heart of the princess, who rejected all the suitors one after the other.

So after a year, the king, a little anxious, asked her to make a decision and choose a husband. The princess replied that she needed to think, and to do so she went to the same park where she had met Ricky with the Tuft in the hope of finding some solitude there. While she walked deeply immersed in her thoughts, she saw various servants carrying cooking pots, torches and fine tablecloths. Curious, she followed them and saw that a magnificent banquet was

being laid out in a clearing in the middle of the park. Astounded, the princess asked a maid the reason for the great banquet that was being prepared. "We are getting ready for the wedding of Prince Ricky with the Tuft," she replied.

It was only at that moment that the princess remembered that, exactly a year ago, she had promised to marry Prince Ricky. At the time, foolish as she was, she had not realized the consequences of her decision, but now she knew she could have chosen any man as her husband!

She decided to rush back to the palace, but on the way she ran into Ricky with the Tuft. "Here I am, my lady, as I promised. I hope you have come here because you are keeping your word, to make me the happiest man in the world by giving me your hand in marriage," said the young man.

"I must confess that I have not made a decision yet and I am afraid that it will not be the one that you are hoping for. I am sure that you will understand. You will know why, when I was still stupid, I did not hesitate and agreed to marry you. I hope you will not consider me superficial if now I have doubts. If you wanted to marry me, you should not have made me intelligent."

"Allow me to protest, because I love you with all my heart and my happiness depends on your decision! And tell me now: apart from my appearance, is there anything else you do not like?" Ricky asked. "Nothing: you are witty, interesting, and wise…," the princess replied. "That being the case I am happy again, because you can easily make me the most handsome of men."

"But how is that possible?" the princess asked. "It is easy," Ricky with the Tuft replied. "You simpy have to love me so much that you to want it to be so. The same fairy who gave me the gift of making the person I love intelligent, also gave you the gift of making the person you love beautiful."

"In that case I wish with all my heart that you should become my husband!"

As soon as the princess had said this, Ricky with the Tuft suddenly appeared in her eyes to be the most handsome man the world. According to some, this change had not taken place because of the fairy's gift, but because of her love for the prince: this enabled the princess to see the beauty of the man concealed behind his appearance. The fact is that the princess's decision was also welcomed by the king and so the next day their wedding was celebrated, marking the beginning of many years of happiness for the young couple.

Donkey Skin

Once upon a time there was a king so powerful and so beloved that he could certainly say that he was the happiest of all monarchs. His castle was overflowing with treasures, the strangest of which was undoubtedly the donkey that with a single touch of his hooves could transform straw into gold! But the king did not consider this exceptional animal his most precious possession: as he often said, his wife was his only treasure.

But it happened that one sad day the queen fell ill. None of the treatments helped and so, knowing that her end was nigh, she called the king and said: "I know that the country will need a new queen. But promise me that she will have the same blue eyes as me, so that when you look at her you will think of me."

On hearing these words the king started crying, and he promised he would do what she asked. But after his wife had died he refused to take another wife in spite of his counselors' insistence. Even if he had wanted to comply with the queen's wishes there was not a single woman in the kingdom who had the same wonderful blue eyes as her, except for their little daughter. So the king had an idea: he would give his adopted daughter in marriage to the wisest of his counselors and he would leave the throne to her so that she would become the new queen.

But when the time came to celebrate the marriage, the princess realized that the man she was about to marry was not only very old but also very hard-hearted. In despair, she tried to postpone the wedding by asking her father for three dresses: a golden one like the sun, a silver one like the moon and a third one sparkling like the stars. She thought these gowns would be impossible to make and that meanwhile she would be able to make the king

change his mind. But in the course of just a few months the seamstresses managed to produce the three magnificent garments requested and the king proudly showed them to the girl. "Is there anything else you would like?" he asked her. "I would like a cloak made from the skin of your magic donkey," the princess replied, knowing that her father was very fond of the animal and certain that he would never agree to sacrifice it. But, without hesitation, the monarch had the donkey killed and ordered a cloak to be made from its skin. This he presented to his daughter saying: "Here is what you asked for: tomorrow we shall celebrate the wedding."

The princess decided that the only way to escape from such a terrible fate was to leave the palace. So, during the night, while everyone was asleep, she folded the three gossamer-like gowns small enough to fit in a nutshell, then, having blackened her face, hands and feet with soot, she put on the cloak made of donkey skin and left the palace.

She walked for days without anyone daring to approach her because of her strange appearance, until she arrived at a farmhouse. The owner welcomed her warmly and gave her food; then, because he needed someone to do the chores and look after the goats, he asked her to stay and work for him in exchange for a small, dark closet that from then on would be her room. Several months elapsed without any interesting happening and by now the princess had become resigned to her life of hard work and lowly chores, as well as to the nickname of "Donkey Skin" that the other servants had given her because of the ugly cloak she wore.

But one day, sitting near the fountain where the goats usually drank, she saw her reflection in the water. She was so horrified to see how dirty and disheveled she looked that she immediately took a decision: once a week she

would spoil herself. Shut up in her little room, she would wear her three wonderful dresses one after the other. It was a holiday and Donkey Skin had decided to wear her sunshine dress when the king's son, returning from a hunting trip, stopped at the farmhouse and asked for food and shelter for himself and his retinue.

The owner of the farm ordered the cooks to prepare a meal worthy of His Majesty and to serve it the royal guests. In the meantime the prince, hungry and bored, decided to wander through the courtyards and stables.

And so it was that he discovered a dark corridor at the end of which he saw a closed door under which shone a ray of light. Curious, he looked through the keyhole and what he saw left him breathless!

In that tiny room he had a glimpse of the most beautiful girl he had ever seen, but when she turned round and the prince could see her incredible blue eyes, he slowly stepped back, convinced that he was the victim of a powerful spell: how else could the feelings he was already feeling for this girl be explained?

From that day on he lost his appetite and was unable to sleep: he was determined to find this girl. He summoned the owner of the farmhouse to court but his explanation did not help at all: he maintained that only a young servant, called Donkey Skin, lived in that cubby-hole. Unpretentious, she was always dirty, but she cooked the most delicious cakes. If he wanted, he could have one brought to His Majesty. The prince bitterly regretted that he had not knocked on the door that evening, and this feeling was so strong that it made him fall seriously ill. He had simply lost the will to live.

A few days later, the cake prepared for him by Donkey Skin arrived. Eager to please the prince, the owner of the farmhouse had ordered Donkey Skin to make one of her cakes as soon as he got home.

The princess had only just had the time to hide her sunshine dress under her usual dirty cloak before running to the kitchen. While she was mixing the flour and the eggs, a thin gold ring slipped off her finger, so ending up inside the cake.

The prince had only taken a small mouthful when he nearly choked: he immediately recognized the little ring he had choked on! He had seen it on the finger of the beautiful fairy who had so bewitched him in the farmhouse! The queen noticed from the way the prince looked at the ring that he was madly in love and, understanding the cause of his illness at last, she asked the name of the girl who was making him suffer so.

So he had to tell her that he did not know: "But of one thing I am certain: this ring is so small that it would only fit the girl I have seen. Help me find her and I shall marry her!"

The queen ordered the heralds to summon all the girls in the kingdom to present themselves at court. The first to arrive were the princesses, then the duchesses, marchionesses and baronesses; but not one of these noble young women could slip the ring on her finger, however hard she tried. The monarchs decided that their son's happiness was more important than the nobility of his future wife, so they summoned the seamstresses, chambermaids and cooks until every single woman in the kingdom had tried on the ring. "Has the girl called Donkey Skin who made the cake been summoned?" the prince asked. Everyone laughed and replied that she not been asked because she was too dirty and miserable-looking to be the right girl. "Go and fetch her immediately," the king said: "It shall never be said that I did not do everything in my power!" So, laughing, the pages went to the farmhouse to fetch the girl. Having lost her precious ring, Donkey Skin had already thought that the ring described by the heralds was hers, and in her heart she hoped it was!

As soon as she heard the knock on the door, quick as a flash she put on her moonshine gown, concealing it beneath her cloak. Dressed like this, the pages took her back to the prince who said to her: "Show me your hand." It was hard to guess who was the most amazed among the king and queen, the pages and the courtiers when they saw, under the donkey skin cloak, a delicate finger onto which the ring slipped without any difficulty. The princess then let her cloak fall to grond, so revealing her enchanting beauty to everyone who was there. The prince immediately recognized her and immediately asked her to marry him. But she told him her story and said she could not marry without the consent of her father, for which reason he would be the first to be invited to the wedding. When he arrived at court and saw the daughter he thought he had lost, he started crying for joy and immediately gave his consent for the marriage. The wedding was celebrated that very very day and the two young people lived happily ever after.

The Fairies

Once upon a time there was a widow who had two daughters. The elder girl looked so much like her mother, in both character and appearance, that all the inhabitants of the village reacted in the same way at the sight of one or the other: after noticing their incredible resemblance with amazement, they would immediately find some excuse to avoid them both. The two of them were so unpleasant and arrogant that it was impossible to have a conversation with them. On the other hand, the younger daughter had inherited her father's sweet and gentle nature, and ever since she was a little baby she had been loved by everyone for her smile, her sweetness and her dazzling beauty.

Unfortunately, because those who resemble each other are always mutually attracted, it became obvious to everyone that the mother very much favored her elder daughter and was growing increasingly distant from her younger one, whom she treated with contempt and forced to do all the chores in the house without ever allowing her a break. One of the younger daughter's hardest tasks was to go to the fountain, a long way away from the house, carrying a heavy earthenware jug to fill with fresh water for the family. However, thanks to her unshakable optimism, she did not mind this onerous task, taking advantage of the walk in the spring to pick flowers and enjoy some quiet moments in the wood, reading a few pages from the book she always had with her.

But one frosty winter morning, she had to run to the fountain to keep warm and to get back home as soon as possible. It was on that day that she had an unexpected encounter.

While she was filling her jug, an old lady approached, an old peasant woman dressed in threadbare, tattered clothes who asked her to give her a little water to drink. "Of course," the young girl replied, holding up the jug so that she could drink more easily. Then, seeing the old rags she was wearing, the young girl took pity on her and offered her cloak to the poor woman.

"Thank you but I cannot accept. You have already been too kind," the old woman replied. "Much more so than I expected, in fact," she added, as her voice and appearance changed.

The young girl was dumbfounded as she watched the amazing transformation: in a few moments no trace of the old peasant woman was left. Standing in front of her now was the most beautiful woman she had ever seen, smiling at her, her hair and eyes the color of ice. "Who are you?" the young girl said in a whisper. "A fairy, my dear. I have come here from the magic kingdom to show my sisters that they are wrong: they claim there is no longer any kindness in the world of humans, while I believe that there are still people who are good and generous towards their fellows, and you have surely proved that I am right. To reward your kindness I shall give a gift: every time you pronounce a word, a flower or a precious stone will come forth from your mouth."

As soon as the young girl returned home after her amazing encounter, she was harshly scolded by her mother: "May I know where you have been?"

"I am so sorry, I did not mean to be late but something happened…" Then before she could continue, three roses, two pearls and four large diamonds fell out of her mouth. "What have you done? Where did you find these jewels?" her mother asked excitedly as she picked up the precious stones. The girl told her about her amazing encounter, thus releasing another cascade of jewels, this time rubies, that piled up at her feet. Losing no time, the mother rushed to call her elder daughter: "Quick, you must go to the fountain immediately! There you will find an old peasant woman, treat her kindly and…"

"To the fountain?" she replied exasperated, "I don't think so!"

"Do as I tell you! You too must receive the same extraordinary gift as your sister." Grumbling, the elder sister dressed to go the fountain: she put on her warmest clothes and took the most beautiful silver jug she could find in the house. She had only just arrived at the fountain when she saw a woman coming out of the wood; she was magnificently dressed, with eyes and hair the color of ice. She asked her for some water to drink.

It was the same fairy who had already appeared to her sister, but she had decided to present herself to the surly sister without being disguised as the old peasant woman the mother had spoken about. So the ill-mannered girl did not recognize her and replied rudely: "I am not here to give you drink! If you want water, go and get it yourself: I'm sure you are perfectly capable of doing that. Now get out of my way and let me look for the old beggar woman."

The fairy was not put out but raised her hand: "Before you go, I would like to give you a gift that is perfectly suited to you: with each word you speak, a toad will come out of your mouth." She had just returned home when her mother rushed to her and asked: "So, my daughter, how did it go?"

"How did it go!" her daughter replied rudely, spewing out three toads.

"What? It is all your sister's fault!" the mother screamed as she lunged at her younger daughter, who only just had time to get her cloak and flee into the wood. It was under her favorite tree that she met the king's son, back from hunting. The prince noticed her and walked towards her; he asked what she was doing alone in the forest and why she was crying.

"I cannot go back home," the girl replied, as three emeralds and two diamonds fell onto the snow.

After her initial surprise, the prince begged her to explain what had happened. She told him every detail.

Listening to her speak and finding out how kind she was, the king's son fell in love with her. So he took the girl back to the palace and presented her to his father who, realizing that such a gift was worth more than any dowry a noble bride could bring, gave his consent for the prince to marry the girl. As for the other sister, she was so ashamed of the fairy's disgusting gift that the wretched creature fled from the village and disappeared forever in the woods.

Bluebeard

Once upon a time there was a man as rich as he was ugly. He owned palaces, lands, stables of thoroughbred horses and chests filled with gold coins, but his appearance was hideous, and it was certainly not improved by his blue beard. Because he wanted to get married, he had already asked for the hand of many young girls, but all of them had refused him, both because of his appearance, and also because of what was said about him: it was rumored that he had already been married several times, but no one knew where his previous wives had ended up. In the same city as Bluebeard, as he was known, lived a lady of noble origins, but she was now living in poverty. She had four children: the two girls were extremely beautiful and the two boys dreamed of becoming knights, but with no money to buy captain's commissions they had no chance of that. So when Bluebeard knocked on the door and asked for the hand of one of her daughters, the woman hesitated: the wealth of the man would be invaluable for the two girls, but at the same time she did not feel like uniting one of her beloved daughters with a person so scary and mysterious. It was the young girl who resolved her doubts, deciding to accept the proposal. She was very young and a little naive, but she was eager to enjoy the luxuries and wealth promised to her by that particular man whenever they met. The wedding was celebrated with great pomp and the new bride took pride in showing off the marvelous palace in which she now lived to her friends.

In the event her husband seemed to be kinder than had been expected and her brothers were not afraid of him.

Then one day Bluebeard announced that he had to leave the house on business. But she would be allowed to continue inviting her friends.

"I will give you the keys to all the doors, all the chests and all the cupboards," he said, taking a jingling bunch of keys out of his pocket. "Spend the money I will leave you as you like; rummage in the cupboards, take what you want from the pantry. But remember: you must on no account go through the door that is at the end of the corridor that is opened by this gold key. Woe betide you if you go into this room: you will bitterly regret it!" This last phrase, of course, simply aroused his wife's curiosity: what could be hidden in that little room?

As soon as Bluebeard had left, the young girl invited her sister and all her friends to visit her. She also left a message with her two brothers, but they told her that they would only be able to come the following day. "Too bad for you!" thought their sister, "You will miss a lovely evening." And so it was: the friends enjoyed themselves tremendously, exploring the rooms and the cupboards, shrieking with delight whenever they came upon new, luxurious clothes, chests full of jewelry and trunks filled with precious silks. In the end no room was left unvisited apart from the forbidden one. The young girl had not given it a single thought all evening, but when her friends had left and her sister was asleep, she went downstairs to the floor below. She approached the forbidden door, then hesitated for a second as she remembered what her husband had said, but in the end she could not resist her curiosity. She put the key in the lock, turned it slowly, opened the door and… screamed!

In the middle of the room was a large axe and piled in a corner were the bodies of several women with their heads chopped off: Bluebeard's vanished wives! Appalled, the young wife clapped her hands to her eyes so as to hide the horrible scene, but in doing so she dropped the gold key onto the ground and it ended up in a pool of blood. She picked it up and fled to her bedroom where she took refuge, trembling from head to toe. When she took the key out of her pocket to put it with the others, she saw that it was stained with blood.

Badly frightened, she tried to wipe it clean, but the key was certainly bewitched because no sooner were the marks removed than they appeared again in the same places. Terrified, the young girl thought of waking her sister and escaping from the palace, but at that very moment Bluebeard returned. The young wife pretended to be asleep so that he would not ask her anything, but the morning afterwards, as soon she came down for breakfast, he interrogated her: "Have you used the key that I forbade you to use?" he asked in a threatening voice.

"N-no, husband of mine," the girl replied, trembling.

"Good, now give it back to me." His wife handed him the key with trembling hands and at once Bluebeard noticed that it was stained. "Why is there blood on this key?"

"I don't know."

"Well, I do!" said the man fiercely. "You have disobeyed me and gone into the little room. Therefore I will put you back in there, and this time for ever, because you will join the other women who were as inquisitive as you." Hearing these words the poor young girl went pale and dropped to her knees: "Forgive me!" she sobbed. "I won't tell anyone what I have seen, believe me!"

"Believe you? You had a chance, but you deceived me, like all the others. I cannot trust you. Don't say anything: come with me because your last hour has come!" Bluebeard rose threateningly and tried to grab the girl by her hair, but she managed to escape and ran upstairs, where her sister was, while the man laughed: "You cannot hide for ever! Now I will go and sharpen my axe and then I will come and get you!"

"My darling sister, help me!" begged the young girl in tears. "Our brothers should be arriving this morning: I beg you to go to the top of the tower and see if you can see them, then call out and ask them to hurry!"

Her sister Anne went quickly to the top of the tower while the young bride waited with her heart in her mouth. Meanwhile Bluebeard, having sharpened his axe, began yelling: "Come down at once or I'll come and get you!"

"All right, I'm coming," the young girl replied, then she anxiously asked her sister: "Can you see anyone?"

"No one!" her sister answered. "Only the grass waving in the breeze."

"I'm tired of waiting," Bluebeard yelled from the floor below. "If you don't come down, I'm coming up!"

"No! I'm coming!" the bride answered, crying. And again she asked her sister: "And now? Don't you see anyone?"

"A cloud of dust, wait! Oh no, it's the sheep going to the pasture."

At that moment they heard the heavy footsteps of Bluebeard who was climbing the steps of the staircase. Arriving at the door, he began to hit it with the axe, since he had failed to open it with a kick, while the bride asked one last time: "Sister, do you see anyone?"

"I see… I can see two horsemen! Yes! They are our brothers!" she replied before calling out to the two young men to hurry up. They burst into the courtyard, ran up the steps two at a time and reached the room not a moment too soon, because Bluebeard was pulling the girl by her hair and dragging her towards the terrible room. The young men threw themselves upon him with their swords drawn and a moment later he lay dead upon the ground, while their sister, on her knees, did not know whether to laugh or cry.

But time heals everything and so the terrible fear passed. His wife inherited all Bluebeard's possessions and with these she could give a dowry to her sister and help her two brave brothers have a future as knights, while Bluebeard had the end that every scoundrel deserves: he was completely forgotten.

Sleeping Beauty

Once upon a time there were a king and queen, rulers of a country far away, over which they reigned with kindness and generosity. They had been married for many years, but they had no children, and although they had long hoped one day to have a child, the couple's wish had never come true.

At last one day their dream was fulfilled and the queen gave birth to a baby girl, who was named Aurora, like the goddess of the dawn, because they soon discovered that the little creature could fill their lives with light. Even the court seemed to be lit up by the child's smile and, a little later, frantic preparations were being made for the solemn ceremony that was to be held in the castle in honor of the little girl. Every corner of the building was swept and polished by the servants, who also made a hundred guest rooms ready. A week before the ceremony the cooks began kneading, chopping and roasting, and the waiters polished the gold tableware reserved for the most important guests.

Hundreds of invitations were written by hand in gold ink and the fastest riders delivered them to the four corners of the kingdom, but it was the king himself who wrote the invitations for those who were closest to his heart, for the fairies who lived in the kingdom, so that they could be godmothers to the child. The king invited seven fairies, but originally there were eight sisters of the magical woods. There was also the old fairy of the mountain, who no one remembered any more, because for decades she had lived alone in her cave, devoting herself to the study of the black arts.

Eventually the day of the long-awaited ceremony arrived, as did the guests who began entering the castle from the first light of dawn.

During the party, the guests came up to the cradle to show the baby the gifts that they had brought. Finally the fairy godmothers approached and gave Aurora the most precious things imaginable, endowing her with the greatest virtues through their spells. But when the last fairy came to offer the child her gift of happiness, a gust of wind threw open the doors of the castle and dense black smoke invaded the hall, at the center of which the eighth fairy appeared: the old mountain witch, who was angry and offended by the fact that she had not been invited. "What's going on? Who are you?" asked the king, rushing to hold Aurora, who had burst into tears at the sight of the old woman.

"This is the girl you did not want me to know?" said the old woman, pointing at little Aurora with her wand.

"This is our daughter," said the king, "Who are you?"

"I am a much more powerful sorceress than these fairies will ever be and I cannot stand being ignored: it is an unacceptable insult."

"I'm sorry that you have taken offence," said the king, "I pray you, please sit down next to us. I hope you can forgive us."

"Of course, Your Majesty, but only if I myself can give the little princess a gift," said the sorceress with a mischievous smile. Then she lifted her wand, pointed it at the girl and said, "When the princess turns eighteen she will prick her finger with a needle and die." Having said this, the cruel fairy wrapped herself in a black cloud and disappeared as quickly as she had come, leaving the king and queen desperate and the whole court terrified.

When the smoke had cleared, the youngest fairy, who had been interrupted by the arrival of the witch, said shyly: "I may have the solution."

"My powers are not enough to lift the curse laid on the baby, but I have not yet given my gift to the princess and I can use it to lighten the terrible revenge of the witch," she explained. Then she added: "If she is pricked with a needle, Aurora will not die, but she will fall asleep for a hundred years, together with the whole court, and only the kiss of true love will awaken her." The king and queen were relieved, but they also made a decision: for the safety of the princess, from that day on, no one in the kingdom was allowed to keep needles and spindles in the house. "This will surely protect our daughter," said the king, embracing the queen and the baby.

Years passed without anything unusual happening. As the fairies had predicted, the princess grew up and became a kind, cheerful girl, happy and inquisitive. Unfortunately it was exactly this last characteristic that got her into trouble, just as the court was preparing a big party to celebrate her eighteenth birthday. Waiting for the party to begin, Aurora was bored and she began to wander around the castle. She reached a tall tower, at the top of which she found a room that she had never entered. "How strange, I didn't know there was a room up here!" said the princess as she opened the door. The first thing she saw was an old woman who was spinning with a spindle. "Come in my dear, I'm glad to have some company," said the old woman, inviting her to come closer. "What are you doing here, what is this?" the young girl asked. "It is a spindle, princess. It is used for spinning. Would you like to try it?" Aurora had never seen this device and, curious, she picked it up, but in doing so she pricked her finger and a little drop of blood emerged. Immediately the princess felt weak and tired.

The last thing she heard was the laughter of the old woman, who had turned into the mountain witch and was now rejoicing at having accomplished her revenge, while Aurora and the entire court fell into a magic, deep sleep. Gradually the castle was surrounded by an impenetrable forest of thorns that encircled and completely covered it, so much so that the flags flying on the roof were no longer visible. Over the years the legend spread throughout the country: the legend of Sleeping Beauty, as the princess was called, waiting in the highest tower of the castle to be saved by a kiss of love, but none of the suitors could ever penetrate the forest of brambles. Finally a young prince arrived in the kingdom eager to take on the challenge, not knowing that on that very day the period of one hundred years established by the spell would be over. When he approached the mass of thorns, he found beautiful flowers that spontaneously moved aside so that he could easily enter the castle.

Looking for the princess, he crossed the large halls where he saw the nobles and their servants lying down, sleeping next to each other. High up on the throne, the king and queen slept embracing each other. The prince passed them by and went up to the little room in which Aurora was sleeping with a sweet smile on her face. Deeply moved, he entered and approached the princess, looked for a long time at her serenely beautiful face, then he came closer to touch her lips with a kiss. In that instant, the room lit up as if the sun of a new dawn was rising. When the rays of light touched the face of the princess, she suddenly blinked and slowly opened her eyes. So Aurora awoke from her deep sleep and, with her, the whole court. From that day, for over a month, festivities took place in the palace to celebrate the awakening of the court and the marriage of Aurora, who was blessed by the spells of her sweet fairy godmothers.

Hans Christian Andersen

Hans Christian Andersen was one of the most important 19th-century authors of fairy tales. Not only did he collect stories from the popular Nordic tradition; they often inspired him to write his own. Profound, original stories enhanced by the magical atmosphere and evocative lights of the North.

Countless original characters – different from any who had been handed down from generation to generation up till that moment – sprang from his pen.

A Little Mermaid who risks her life to save that of her Prince instead of wistful damsels in distress. A little witch in search of a magic tinderbox rather than a cruel old hag plaguing the unlucky hero – though he manages to overcome her in no time…

Turn the pages to find out which of Andersen's other characters face countless unexpected adventures!

The Princess and the Pea

There was once a prince who wanted to marry a princess, but, under the laws of the kingdom, she had to be without doubt a blue-blooded girl, in short, a real princess. So, the prince decided that he would take a long journey in search of a bride. He traveled his kingdom from north to south, from east to west, but without success. He then ventured into foreign lands and distant countries. He met many young women who claimed to be authentic princesses, but none of them really convinced him. There was always something that left him with doubts. With one, it was the way she behaved, with another it was the way she laughed, and with a third it was her bearing that was not regal enough. So the prince, becoming more and more dejected, continued on his journey around the world. Finally, after months and months of wandering in search of the perfect bride, he decided to return alone to his castle.

One evening, the sky began to cloud over and it became increasingly black and threatening. Then the most violent storm for many years burst upon them. The rain fell in cascades, and deafening thunder followed relentlessly on blinding lightning. The roads were deserted, and the people locked themselves up at home, and huddled by their hearths.

Suddenly, and unexpectedly, someone knocked at the door of the castle. When they went to open the door, the king's guards were faced with a trembling girl, her clothes and hair streaming with water. She told them that she was a princess and that she had come from a distant realm. The king and queen looked her over. She certainly didn't look very regal! The queen was suspicious. She thought, "I know a good way to find out if you really are a princess."

Without a word, she went to the room set aside for guests, put a small pea on the bed and covered it with twenty mattresses and twenty thick quilts. Then she went back to the girl, accompanied her to this room, and bade her good night. The princess could not wait to lie down and sleep, but even though she was exhausted from her long and uncomfortable journey, she could not get to sleep. Whichever way she turned, something hard and annoying prevented her from sleeping.

The next morning, she felt even more tired and sore. The king and queen came to her door, asking her if she had slept well. The princess smiled wanly and said, "I'm sorry to say this, but I could not sleep a wink all night. I do not know what it was, but there was something hard in the bed and it gave me painful bruises all over my body! Several times I looked between the sheets to see if there was something, but I found nothing!"

The king and the queen looked satisfied. They had found a true princess for their son. How could they be sure? Simply because only a young woman of royal blood could feel the presence of a pea under twenty mattresses and twenty quilts. Real princesses, you know, have very delicate and sensitive skin.

Now they rushed to the prince and told him what they had discovered: they had finally found the right bride for him!

The young man was very happy because the princess was really beautiful, and her sweet face revealed a kind soul. Without wasting any more time, and this time without any doubt, he asked her to be his wife. The princess happily accepted, and the wedding was celebrated with a lavish ceremony.

And what happened to the pea? It was locked in a case of purest crystal and preserved in the royal museum.

The Little Mermaid

In the ocean, where the water is clear as crystal, where the sea bed lies deepest, stood the castle of the king of the people of the sea. The king was a widower, so it was his aging mother who took care of the princesses, seven lovely mermaids, fascinating creatures whose bodies ended in fish tails. All day, the princesses played in the castle gardens, where each of them had a small flower bed in which she could plant her favorite flowers. One of them planted her flowers in the shape of a whale, another created a floral octopus, but the youngest put in her garden only red flowers and a marble statue of a beautiful young man, which had floated down to them after a shipwreck. The little mermaid was intrigued by the world on land and often asked her grandmother to tell her everything she knew of cities and men!

One evening, the grandmother said to her granddaughters, "When you turn fifteen, you will be allowed to go up to the surface." As each of the sisters' fifteenth birthdays came around, they were one by one allowed to surface. On their return, they told the others what they had seen and heard: the beauty of the sunsets, the moon and the stars, cities full of lights and sounds, the changing of the seasons. On many nights, the little mermaid gazed upwards through the water, and if a shadow passed across the light of the moon, she knew that above her was perhaps a passing whale, or a ship with many men, all unaware of her existence. Finally, the long-awaited birthday arrived. The little mermaid took a deep breath and began kicking upward. As she broke the surface, the sun was setting. When it was almost dark, a great ship passed not far from her, and she could hear music and singing coming from it. The little mermaid swam to a porthole and peered inside. She saw that they were having a party for the young prince, who was also celebrating his birthday that day. All at once, the little mermaid heard the roar of a storm welling up from the

depths of the ocean. Within moments, the waves became bigger and a gale blew up. The ship was lifted by the swell, then it crashed back into the sea. The mast broke and the ship crumpled.

The little mermaid saw the prince disappearing into the waves. She swam as fast as she could, she dived and resurfaced many times until she reached the unconscious young man and, holding his head up out of the water, let the currents carry them away. The next morning the storm had passed. There was no trace of the ship, and the prince was still unconscious. The little mermaid kissed his forehead and watched him for a long time, trying to remember where she had seen him before. Then she remembered the marble statue in her garden. The young man looked very much like it! She hoped against hope that he would live. Then she saw the coast before her. On a promontory stood a magnificent building. A grand staircase ran down to the sea, where there was a small creek leading to a white beach. She swam to it and laid the prince on the sand. When she saw some people approaching, she hid and sang a sweet song to attract their attention. That enchanting voice was the first sound that the prince heard when he awoke. The moment the prince and his rescuers moved away, the little mermaid felt a great sadness come over her, so she dived into the water and returned home. Many times after that, she swam back up to the beach where she had left the prince, but she never once saw him, and she returned home each time sadder than the last. Her sisters begged her to tell them the cause of such sadness, so the little mermaid told them every detail of her first trip to the surface. "Maybe I can help you," said her oldest sister, "I know where to find the prince's palace! Come with me." When they arrived at the royal palace, the little mermaid gasped: she had never seen such a marvelous building! It was made of a shiny yellow stone, had large marble staircases, and golden domes rose up from the roof. The little mermaid returned there many times, edging closer and closer, and she learned not to fear

humans any more. In fact, she wished more and more to live among them. There was so much of their world that she would like to learn about, but one thought, more than any other, stayed with her from the moment she saved the prince. So, one day, she asked her grandmother, "If you save a drowning man from death, will he live forever?" "No, my dear, men also die," replied the older mermaid. "But unlike us, who turn into sea foam, humans possess a soul that continues to live and climbs up to the shining stars, to beautiful places that we can never know!"

"I'd give a hundred of the years that I have yet to live to be like a human just for one day! Grandmother, is there nothing I can do to have a soul?" she asked.

Her grandmother said, "If a man loved you more than anything in the world and married you. Then, part of his soul would enter your body and you would be able to take part in human happiness. But, little one, you have to stop dreaming about the world of men! Those fools would never welcome you! There is something we consider beautiful that is thought horrible on terra firma: our fish tail. For them, those strange props which they call legs and feet are beautiful. Now, let's see your lovely smile: tonight there is a ball at court. Let's go!" concluded her grandmother, taking her hand.

The throne room was a wonderful sight to behold! Thousands of huge shells, pink and green as grass, were lined up on all sides, and in the middle dolphins danced and mermaids sang sweetly. The little mermaid sang better than anyone, and for a moment she felt happy, but immediately her thoughts turned back to the prince. Quietly, she slipped out of the castle, sure she would never give up the love she felt for him. "This is what I'll do!" she said to herself, herself. "I'll go and visit the sea witch. I have always been so afraid of her, but she's the only one who can help me!" Determined, she went to the cave where the witch lived. She had never been there before. Nothing grew there: no algae or coral. There

was only the gray sandy sea bed, and currents that swallowed up all they took hold of. Beyond these terrible whirlpools was the witch's cave, guarded by hundreds of octopuses, which wrapped themselves around anything that approached. The little mermaid stopped, uncertain. Her heart was pounding with fear, but she thought of the prince and screwed up her courage. She tied back her long hair, so that the octopuses couldn't get hold of her, then passed quickly between the horrible creatures. So she came into the presence of the witch, who told her, "I know what you want: to get rid of your fish tail and have in its place two props so that you can walk like a human, so that the prince will fall in love with you... You must be crazy! Still, I'll make you a potion. You must swim up to the beach and drink it before the sun rises. Then your tail will turn into what humans call 'legs'. But remember," added the witch. "Once you have been transformed into a woman, you can never go back to being a mermaid! If you do not find the prince's love, you will never have an immortal soul, and if he marries another, your heart will break with the pain and you will become foam! Are you sure that this is what you want?"

"I'm sure," replied the little mermaid without any hesitation.

"Very well, but you must pay me, and the cost is not small. You have the most beautiful voice of all the inhabitants of the sea and I want it for myself."

"I accept!" exclaimed the little mermaid. The witch gave her the magic potion, taking her voice as payment. The little mermaid passed through the swarm of octopuses and saw in the distance her father's castle. The grand ballroom was dark now. There's no doubt that if she had known what was going to happen she would have stopped right then! As she swam to the surface, she felt that her heart would break. The sun had not yet risen when she reached the beach. She gazed one last time on her long, shiny tail, then drank the fiery potion. Immediately, she felt an unimaginable heat so intense that she fainted. When the sun rose, she woke up and saw before her none other than the prince, and he was staring at her with a worried frown. The little mermaid looked down and saw that her fish tail was gone. Now she possessed the most beautiful white legs that any girl had ever had! The young man asked her who she was. She looked at him kindly, but could not say a word. He helped her up. For the first time, and not without much pain and difficulty, the little mermaid tried to walk on those strange fins called 'feet'. The girl was very welcome at the palace. She received great care and attention. At the banquet that took place that evening in the throne room, she sat at the royal table. Graceful young women danced and sang before the prince, and the mermaid joined their dance, amazing everyone with her grace.

From that day on, the girl and the prince were inseparable. Together they rode and walked through the woods, sharing long silences filled with emotion.

For the little mermaid, walking was terribly painful, and every step felt like a knife piercing her small feet. So, at night, when no one was looking, she would go to the seashore to seek relief in the cool water. One night, her sisters came to the shore to greet her, singing softly and telling her how much everyone missed her.

The young mermaid was greatly saddened, but this was the life she had decided to live, beside the prince, who loved her more and more every day, and who every day wanted more and more to enjoy her silent company.

Often, he told her that she reminded him of the girl who had saved him the night of the storm, the only one that he would have wanted at his side for life. Imagine the despair of the young woman who could not tell him that it was she had who had saved him from the waves and from certain death! One day the prince said sadly, "I have to leave. I have to meet my future wife," and then, seeing the girl's shocked expression, he added, "I do not want to be separated from you either! Come with me. You are not afraid to go to sea, are you?" That evening the two young people waited on the deck of a ship as the sun went down. "My father has been planning this marriage for months! He agreed to wait until I found the girl whose voice I dream of, but now I understand that I see her only in my dreams. And since I have known you, I cannot help but imagine her with your face. If only we could choose who to marry..." he whispered. He moved closer to the little mermaid and placed a kiss on her lips, then, turning for one last, sad look, he went below decks. As night fell, the little mermaid's sisters came to the surface and swam to the ship, singing.

"Little sister, come home," they begged. But she shook her head, her eyes full of tears. "Do you love him so much?" her eldest sister asked. She nodded in si-

lence. This was her place, even if she could not prevent the marriage that would end all her hopes and, indeed, her life.

The next morning, the ship sailed into port. There was a triumphant welcome, and a succession of balls and parties followed one another, but the princess only arrived a few days later. She was very beautiful, her skin was delicate and bright, and her beautiful blue eyes were smiling and full of confidence. "It's you!" exclaimed the prince, "You're the one who saved me from the storm." The little mermaid felt her heart breaking. The morning after the wedding she would be dead, turned into sea foam. The following day, the ceremony was celebrated solemnly, then the couple boarded the ship, and were saluted with the roar of cannon. That night, everyone made merry, and the sailors sang and danced for a long time. Even the little mermaid joined the dance, moving with incomparable grace. The pain in her feet cut like sharp knives, but she paid no attention. The pain in her heart was greater. She knew that this was the last time she would see the man for whom she had left her home, for whom she had given up her beautiful voice, for whom she had suffered daily torment without end. This was the last night she would breathe the same air. She stared into the deep sea and up at the starry sky. Eternal night without thoughts or dreams awaited, because she had no soul, nor could she obtain one. Finally, silence fell on the ship. The little mermaid looked eastward, and saw the red glow of dawn. The first ray of sunlight

would kill her. Now she saw her sisters appear among the waves. They were as pale as she was and their beautiful long hair no longer played in the wind. "We've sold our hair to the witch, in return for helping you," they said. "She gave us this dagger. Before the sun rises, you must bury it in the prince's heart. When his warm blood bathes your feet, they will turn back into a fish tail and you will become a mermaid again. Then you can live out your three hundred years of life before you become salty foam. Do it quickly! Soon the sun will rise, and you will die."

The little mermaid went into the tent where the couple were sleeping and saw the beautiful bride lying with her head on the prince's chest. She leaned toward him and kissed his forehead. In the sky, the light of dawn was brightening. She looked at the knife and then once again at her beloved prince. Desperate, she threw the knife far away into the waves, then jumped into the water and felt her body melting into the foam. The sun rose high above the sea but the little mermaid did not feel as though she was dying. The sun was shining wonderfully, and around her flew creatures that were beautiful and ethereal. Their voices sang a melody so sweet and spiritual that no human ear could hear it. In the same way, no human eye could see them. Light and lovely, they were flying in the air without wings. The little mermaid saw that now she had a body just like theirs, and that with the same lightness she was rising ever higher above the foam. "Where am I going?" she asked, and she heard that her own voice sounded sweet and spiritual just like that of the others. "To the daughters of the air!" they answered her. "As you know, mermaids do not have an immortal soul, and cannot obtain one unless they win the love of a human! The daughters of the air don't have an immortal soul either, but they can win one with good works. We are flying to hotter climes to bring relief and refreshment when the torrid air oppresses and kills men. With perseverance, we continue our mission for three hundred years, and we obtain an immortal soul, forever enjoying the eternal happiness of men. You, poor little mermaid, you have wished with all your heart. You, like us, have suffered and endured, and you came to the world of the creatures of the air. Now, if you do good deeds you may win an immortal soul in three hundred years!"

The little mermaid lifted her transparent arms towards the sun and she felt tears in her eyes. Below her, the ship awoke, and came back to life. She saw that the prince and his beautiful bride were searching for her. They looked sadly at the foam, as if they knew she had thrown herself into the waves. Invisible, she kissed the bride on the forehead, smiled at the prince and soared up with the daughters air to where pink clouds floated in the sky. "In three hundred years we will enter the kingdom of God!" whispered one of them. "We may even reach there sooner. Without being seen, we enter the houses of men where there are children. Every time we find a good child who makes his parents happy and deserves their love, the Lord shortens the period of our trial. The child does not know when we come into the house, but when we smile at him for joy one of those years flies away. But if we find a bad and naughty child, then we weep with pain and every tear increases our trials by a day!"

The Tin Soldier

There was once an old man who loved to make toys using anything that came to his hand. One day he found a lead ladle abandoned in a corner, and he decided he would make a tiny toy army. So he made twenty-five toy soldiers. Each one had a rifle on his shoulder, wore a smart red and turquoise uniform, and with a fierce and determined look seemed all ready to march. The old man laid them carefully in a box and put them on sale.

Imagine the surprise and joy of the little boy who received them that Christmas!

Right away, he took them out of the box and put them in a row on the table to admire them better. They were all the same, except one, who was standing perfectly erect like others, despite having only one leg. You see, he was the last soldier to be made and there had not been quite enough lead left to finish him off. The child became attached to this one immediately, and the soldier soon became his favorite toy.

On the table with the small army there were many other playthings, but what stood out more than any other toy was a fantastic cardboard castle, complete with a fortified tower. Through its windows you could see the ballroom, richly decorated for the evening. In front of the castle, surrounded by lovely trees, there was a lake, set with a small mirror, on which swam tiny white swans made of wax.

But what attracted your attention was the figure of a little girl with perfect features, standing in front of the main entrance. Like the castle, she was made of cardboard, but she was wearing a beautiful dress and a light veil of blue silk ribbon encircled her shoulders like a scarf.

At the center of it shone a silver star, which lit up her beautiful face. She was holding her arms up over her head, and she was balancing on the tip of one foot.

The other leg, stretched upward, was partially hidden by a long skirt. She was a ballerina. As soon as he was taken out of the box, the soldier's attention was attracted by the beautiful maiden and, looking carefully, he thought that, like himself, she had only one leg. Determined to meet her, he hid himself behind a snuff box that lay on the table among the toys, hoping the child would forget him. Indeed, come the evening, the boy hastily put the other soldiers away in the box, without realizing that he had forgotten his favorite one. It was late now, and everyone went to bed. Silence fell over the house, but in this room a great party started, and its guests were all toys. They all laughed and played happily, some played soccer, some played hide and seek, some played blind man's buff; all but the poor soldiers, locked up in their box. In all this confusion, only two figures remained motionless, almost indifferent to fuss: the dancer on her point with her arms raised high and our tin soldier, erect and composed in his uniform. He never looked away from girl, although he could not find the courage to approach her and talk to her.

At midnight, they heard a sharp click, the snuffbox lid opened and out jumped an evil imp. He was also madly in love with the dancer and it took only glance to realize that he had a rival. Mad with jealousy, he arrogantly called out to the soldier, but he did not answer, remaining motionless. This made the imp angry, and he swore that he would

get even. He shouted at the soldier, "You'll see: you won't get away with it! I'll find a way to make you pay. No one takes my place near the beautiful girl. Watch your back! My revenge will come when you least expect it and it will be terrible!"

The following morning, when the child awoke, he saw the soldier out of his box and placed him on the window sill. We will never know whether the evil imp cast a spell, or whether it was just a gust of wind, but the fact is that the

window suddenly flew open and the soldier fell out. He ended up stuck head first between the cobblestones, his one leg up and his bayonet down, and the tip of his helmet driven into the ground.

The boy ran into the street to look for him, but the carriages passing at great speed and the people who thronged the sidewalk hid him from view, and so the poor child was forced to return home, saddened by the loss of his favorite toy. Meanwhile, the first drops of rain started to fall. First, drizzle, and then ever harder, until it turned into a violent downpour, that flooded the streets in a flash.

The storm had just finished when two boys saw the soldier still stuck between the cobblestones. One of the two had an idea: to float him along the rivulets of water that were running into the drains. So, they made a paper boat and put the soldier in it. As soon as they launched their fragile craft on the water it was sucked into the current and ended up in a dark and dangerous sewer. The poor soldier could not see anything and clung to the boat desperately. All at once, a fat sewer rat appeared and threatened him, demanding that he pay a toll. But the soldier did not answer him and, holding his rifle and bayonet firmly in front of him, he passed safely. He was carried onwards for what seemed an eternity, until, at a certain point, he thought he saw a glimmer of light, and began to hope that this perilous journey would soon come to an end. But his misfortunes were not yet over! The stream on which he was sailing was about to plunge into a wide canal, a drop that for our toy soldier was equivalent to Niagara Falls! The crash was terrible: the boat spun around several times, was swamped with water and capsized. The tin soldier fell into the canal, and his only thought was that he would never see his beloved ballerina again. In that exact moment, a huge fish swallowed him in one bite.

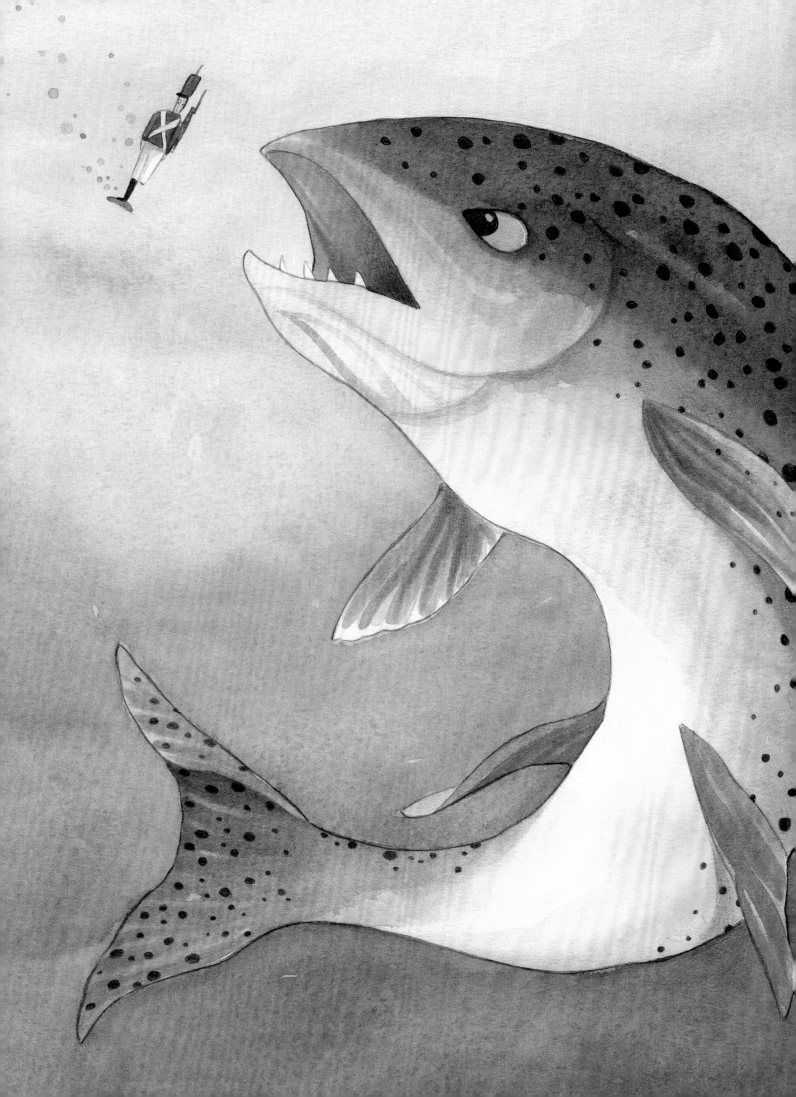

Inside the fish, it was pitch dark and the space was very small.

As luck would have it, soon after, the fish was caught in a fisherman's net, and it was taken to market to be sold.

Fate works in mysterious ways, and, incredibly, the fish was bought by the cook who worked for the little boy's family. Imagine their surprise when the soldier was found in the belly of the fish! Straight away, the child put him back on the table where it had all begun. Everything was in its place, even the sweet ballerina, who was still standing at the entrance of the castle, where nearby the regal swans swam on the mirror lake. The soldier was happy. He looked on the girl with love, and this time she looked back at him with the same tenderness.

In fact, the ballerina had been very worried when she did not see him lined up with his companions and now at last she felt reassured. But, alas, life, as we have said, never ceases to amaze. It is full of surprises.

Shortly afterwards, one of the younger children, to spite his older brother, seized the soldier and threw him into the fireplace, in the midst of the flames. Perhaps the black imp, angry that his rival had returned, had a hand in it.

All hope was lost: the poor thing felt a terrible heat, the color of his uniform was fading and he could not catch his breath. He looked towards the ballerina with sadness and regret, thinking that they might have spent a long life together if only fate had not been so unkind! The girl returned his look. Her feelings were the same. Once again they were separated!

At that moment, the door burst open and a great gust of wind swept the castle and the ballerina straight into the fire. In a second, the cardboard of which they were made caught fire and a brilliant flame brought an end to their dream. So it was all over?

The following day, as usual, the fireplace was cleaned out, the ashes were collected with a brush and swept into a dustpan.

Thus, unexpectedly, the two were finally together, despite the evil intrigues of the black imp and the twists and turns of capricious fate.

The Emperor's New Clothes

Many years ago, there lived an emperor, who gave so much importance to the beauty and richness of clothes that he spent most of his money on his wardrobe. Nothing mattered more to him than to have the opportunity to show off some new outfit. In the great city in which he lived, it was very busy, and foreigners arrived every day.

One day, a pair of fraudsters arrived. They were posing as skilled weavers who were famous throughout the world, and they boasted that they could weave for the king the most beautiful fabric you could find. Not only would the colors and the design be extraordinarily beautiful, but the clothes made from this fabric would possess unusual properties: they were invisible to the eyes of those who were not capable of the tasks entrusted to them, or who were just very stupid.

"Ah, yes, these would indeed be magnificent clothes," thought the emperor. "With such clothes on, it would be easy to distinguish the clever from the stupid and find out who is not up to the task that I have entrusted to him! I must have these clothes at all costs!"

And so, he gave a fat advance to the two fellows, so that they would lose no time but begin work immediately. They promptly set up two looms and pretended to make a start on the weaving, but in fact the looms were empty. They asked to be supplied with the most precious silk and the finest gold thread, and they popped them into their bags, continuing to work at the empty looms until late into the night.

"I'd like to know where they are with the work," thought the emperor, but it struck him that anyone who was too foolish or who was inadequate to their task would not be able to see the cloth.

He knew that, as far as he was concerned, this was not a problem, but he thought it would be wiser to first send someone else to see how things were going. Now in the city, there was talk of nothing but the wonderful properties of the fabric, and everyone was curious to find out how stupid or incompetent his neighbor was.

"I will send my venerable old prime minister to the weavers. His honesty is unquestionable," thought the emperor. "There is no one better to judge the work, because he is intelligent and always tries to live up to his office."

And the good old prime minister went into the room where the two rogues pretended to work at the empty looms. "God help me!" he thought, opening his eyes wide. "I don't see anything!"

However, he was careful not to say it out loud. The two rascals invited him to come closer, and asked him if he appreciated the beauty of the pattern and the range of colors they were using, pointing here and there at the empty loom.

However hard he tried, the poor prime minister could not see anything and, in anguish, he thought, "Poor me! Am I really so stupid? I never thought to be so, but no one really likes to think that of himself. And what if I am not capable of doing my job? No. I cannot report to the emperor that I cannot see the cloth."

Then one of the two fraudsters asked him, "What do you think?"

"Oh, it's really magnificent!" said the prime minister. "What delicate patterns, what refined colors! I am very impressed by your work and will tell the emperor so!"

"We are so happy!" said the weavers, and began once again to point out the colors and the details of the design. The prime minister listened to them carefully so that he could repeat everything to the emperor, and he did so. The two swindlers asked for more money, more silk, more gold thread to enrich the fabric, and of course it all ended up in their pockets.

Satisfied, they carried on with their deceit, working at the empty loom. Shortly after the visit of the prime minister, the emperor, impatient, sent one of his highest officials to check the quality of the work and its progress. Everything happened in the same way as had happened to the prime minister: the official looked and looked again, but could not see anything, because the loom was completely empty.

"What do you think? The fabric is magnificent, is it not?" asked the two tricksters, showing him the extraordinary quality of a fabric that was not there.

"But, I'm no fool!" thought the official, "And that means that I must not be fit for office. It seems very odd! In any case, it is better that no one finds out." So, he praised the beauty of the fabric that he really could not see, and declared himself fully satisfied.

"It's really gorgeous work!" he reported to the emperor.

And in the city no one spoke of anything other than this magnificent fabric.

In the end, curiosity got the better of him. The emperor wanted to examine the fabric himself, even though it was still on the loom and not completely finished. Accompanied by a large crowd of courtiers, the prime minister and the high official among them, the emperor went to view the work in progress. The two fake weavers were working now with more vigor than ever, but with neither warp nor weft.

"It's wonderful, isn't it, Majesty?" exclaimed the two officials. "Look at the embroidery and the colors. What refinement! What craftsmanship!" So saying they gestured to the empty loom, thinking that the others were able to see the cloth.

"But what are they talking about?" thought the emperor. "I don't see anything! This is terrible! Am I a fool? Or am I not fit to be emperor? This is the worst thing that could happen to me..."

While he was immersed in these thoughts, aloud he said, "Oh, but it's beautiful! It's just to my liking." He went up to the empty loom, pretending to examine the work, unwilling and unable to confess to not seeing anything.

All those who followed him, looked in the direction of the loom and of course saw nothing. But they all said, "Beautiful! Magnificent!" And they advised him to wear his new clothes for the first time in the gala parade at the next festival. The emperor conferred knighthoods upon the two fraudsters, with the title of Weavers of the Imperial House.

The night before the day of the festival, the two rascals stayed up to work, with more than sixteen candles lit, so that everyone could see that they were busy finishing the emperor's new clothes. They pretended to take the cloth from the loom. Then they cut the air with tailor's shears, and they sewed with a needle without thread, and finally announced, "There, the clothes are ready!"

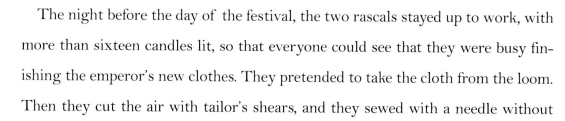

The emperor himself appeared, along with his most illustrious knights, and the two scoundrels, raising their hands in the air, as if displaying something, said, "These are the breeches! Here is the jacket! Here is the train!" and so on. "They are light as a spider's web! It seems as if I'm not wearing anything, but this is definitely their greatest virtue."

All the courtiers nodded with conviction, while not one of them saw anything, because there really wasn't anything to see.

"And now, Majesty, if you would deign to undress, we will help you to put on your new clothes before the mirror," said the villains.

The emperor undressed and the two charlatans pretended to hand him the items one by one, helping him to put them on, pretending to pin to his shoulders something that must be the train, and the emperor turned this way and that before the mirror.

"Majesty, they suit you so well!" everyone exclaimed. "What beautiful design! What colors! It is a gorgeous suit of clothes!"

"Your canopy awaits, Majesty, for you to lead the procession!" announced the master of ceremonies.

"I'm ready," said the emperor, "I really look fine, right?" And once again he turned round in front of the mirror, as if to admire his new suit.

The pages in charge of holding the train, bent down, as if to pick up the cloth from the ground. They walked with hands held out in front of them, because they did not want to let it be known that they saw nothing, much less a train to carry. And so the emperor took his place at the head of the solemn procession, under the large canopy, and all the people rushed into the streets and looked out of the windows, exclaiming, "My, but the emperor's new clothes are so extraordinary! What a beautiful train! How wonderful he looks!" In fact, no one wanted to admit that they could see nothing, and so be judged incompetent or unfit for their jobs. The imperial clothes had never before attracted such admiration.

"But he's got nothing on!" a child suddenly called out.

"My goodness! Hear the voice of innocence!" exclaimed the father, and everyone began to whisper to one another, what the child had said.

"He's got nothing on! A child says that the emperor has nothing on!"

"He's got nothing on!" they were finally all shouting.

The emperor shuddered, for he knew that they were right, but in the meantime he thought, "At this point I have to get through this farce and I have to finish the parade."

So, he squared his shoulders and stepped out with an even more majestic gait, and the pages kept walking, carrying the train that was not there.

The Snow Queen

One day, the devil made a mirror capable of hiding the good and beautiful things that were reflected, showing instead all that was ugly, and when something ugly was reflected, it became uglier still. If there was a good thought, in the mirror it was transmuted into a bad one. The devil traveled all over the world with the mirror, and in the end there was nothing that had not been reflected and deformed. Still not satisfied, he decided to fly to the gates of heaven. He had almost reached the realm of the angels, when the mirror slipped from his hands and plummeted to Earth, where it broke into millions of tiny pieces. Some took flight and were carried all round the world by the wind, and when they got into the eyes of people, they buried themselves deep, so they could see only the worst side of things. Some shards worked their way into people's hearts, turning them to ice.

The two young people at the center of our story lived in a very poor neighborhood and their houses were so close that, where the two roofs met, the gutters joined. It was enough to hop over them to pass from one attic to another. Their parents had hung wooden boxes from the windows and in them they had planted herbs and fragrant roses, and the two friends would sit near them to play. They loved each other very much, and they were inseparable! He was called Kay and she was Gerda. One cold winter's day, Kay's grandmother, to distract them said, "Look! You think these are snowflakes, but to me they seem to be large white bees!"

"Do they, too, have their own queen bee?" asked Kay.

"Certainly!" his grandmother said. "Sometimes she flies over the city and looks in through the windows, which then freeze in the strangest way, as if they were covered with flowers."

One evening, Kay pulled up a chair to the window to watch the snow, and

suddenly he saw two big flakes slide toward him. The largest of these fell into one of the boxes of flowers and began to grow until it turned into a beautiful woman, wrapped in white veils that seemed to consist of a snowstorm. Kay was frightened and jumped down from the chair, while a whirlwind transformed the woman into a huge white bird, which took flight. By the next morning, though, Kay had convinced himself that he had dreamed it. When spring finally returned, the children made a habit of meeting in their own little garden between the roofs. One day, while reading a book, Kay said, "Ouch! I've got something in my eye!" Gerda tried to help him, but she could see nothing. In fact, one of the shards from the magic mirror had got into the child's eye and another had worked its way down to his heart. Soon it would become ice! "Why are you making that face?" Kay rudely asked Gerda, "And now why are you crying?" The girl ran home in tears, while Kay, left alone, realized that he could suddenly see details that he had never noticed before! "That rose has been ruined by worms! The other one's crooked! In fact, those roses are just horrible!" When winter came round again, Kay seemed very happy. One day he stole his grandmother's glasses and, hanging them out of the window he waited for the snowflakes to settle on them. "Look how beautiful, Gerda!" he exclaimed, showing her how, thanks to the lenses, each flake looked larger and just like a flower. Then he ran out of the house with his sled on his back. In the square, the boys were having fun, secretly hitching their sleds to the wagons of the farmers and letting themselves be dragged along. He was playing at this when he came upon a large white sleigh, on which sat a person wrapped in a white fur coat and with her face covered by a hood. The sleigh stopped and Kay took the opportunity to tie his little sled to it. As soon as he had tied the last knot, the sleigh sped off. The driver nodded affectionately to Kay, as if they already knew each other. Unable to untie his sled, the child clung with all his strength and soon they left the city behind. He tried again to untie the rope, but to no avail. Kay was terrified! The snowflakes that were falling grew larger and larger, until it seemed to Kay that he was surrounded by large white birds. Suddenly the sleigh came to a halt. The driver stood up and pushed back her hood, and Kay recognized the woman he had seen out of the window of his room! It was the Snow Queen. She took the child by the hand, made him sit beside her on the sleigh and wrapped him in the hem of her white bear fur. "Are you still cold?" she asked, kissing him on the forehead. Kay shuddered; that kiss was colder than ice! For a moment he seemed almost to die, but then he felt better. When the Snow Queen gave him a second kiss, something terrible happened. Kay forgot little Gerda, and everyone he had left back home. The Queen urged the sleigh into the air and it flew unerringly through the snowstorm that was now raging. As dawn broke, Kay was asleep at the feet of the Snow Queen.

You can imagine how Gerda felt when Kay did not return! She asked everyone in the town if they had seen him, but no one could give her an answer. Some boys remembered seeing him tie his sled to a magnificent sleigh, but their memories were inexplicably confused. In short, no one knew where the boy had gone or who he had gone with. In the end, they said that Kay must have fallen into the frozen river and that she had to resign herself to it. So she stopped looking for him. Gerda wept for a long time over the disappearance of her friend. Then, the cold passed again and spring arrived, bringing with it beautiful warm sunshine. It was to the sun that Gerda turned one morning, as she sat alone, among the roses. "Kay has drowned."

"No, I do not believe it!" answered the sun.

"I tell you he is dead! Gone!" replied Gerda.

"No, we don't believe it!" said the swallows and so, eventually, Gerda too stopped believing it, and she decided to go in search of her friend. She traveled for a long time, questioning the flowers and the stars, but they all answered that they knew nothing.

Months passed, and Gerda found herself alone, far from home amid the cold of winter, but she kept on, trying to stop shivering and shake off her sadness. One day she had stopped to rest by the side of a road when a crow hopped across the snow in front of her. "Caw, caw! Good morning!" he said, and he asked how she came to be all alone in the world. Gerda told the crow what had happened and asked if he had seen Kay.

The bird said, "Could be. I think that a child I met could be little Kay, but certainly he has now forgotten you for the princess."

"He lives with a princess?" asked Gerda.

"Yes. Let me explain! In this kingdom, there is a very clever princess who is terribly bored. One day she thought to herself that if she were not always alone, maybe she would not be so bored. So she decided to find a husband. But she desired a person who could join her in conversation and who would not bore her.

The following day she announced that every handsome young man was invited to the palace and that the one who showed himself the most intelligent would be her husband! A large crowd descended upon the palace, but finding a husband for the princess was not so easy, because everyone became tongue-tied in her presence and not a single one could get a word out!"

"But, Kay?" Gerda asked. "When does he come into it?"

"All in good time!" cried the crow. "It was on the third day that the princess received suitors, when a young boy appeared. His eyes sparkled and he had beautiful long hair, but he was dressed like a peasant."

"It was Kay!" cried Gerda, happily.

"He had a bundle on his back," said the bird.

"That would have been his sled!" said Gerda.

"When he arrived at the palace, he was not at all intimidated and walked quietly into the presence of the princess, who sat on the throne, bored. He had not come to ask for her hand, he said, but only to find out how intelligent she was. He soon learned that she was extraordinary, and she found him extraordinary too."

"I'm certain it was Kay!" exclaimed Gerda. "Can you get me into the palace?"

"It's not possible. The guards would not allow it," said the crow. "But my sister, who works at the palace, knows a little back door which leads to the princess's bedroom."

When the palace lay in darkness, the bird led the girl to a back door, which was ajar. They went in and climbed an imposing staircase, at the top of which they found the tame crow, and she led them to the royal chamber. Gerda went to the bed, lifted a corner of the sheet and saw dark hair. Excited, she called out Kay's name and woke up the prince.

What a disappointment it was to discover that the young man was not Kay! The princess also woke up and demanded to know what was going on. Then the little girl began to cry and told her whole story. Moved, the princess gave Gerda clothes that were both warm and elegant, and placed a golden carriage with the royal crest at her disposal. So the child resumed her journey, but after a while the carriage was attacked by vicious bandits who mistook Gerda for a rich noblewoman and took her prisoner. The child was taken to the bandits' lair where she met their leader's daughter. She was ugly and clumsy, and her ways intimidated Gerda. She showed her the doves that she was holding captive in small cages and her reindeer, tied to the wall with a golden ring through its the nose. Gerda told her story, while the robbers sang and drank around the fire. When everyone was asleep, the doves said, "We have seen little Kay. He was sitting in the carriage of the Snow Queen, heading for Lapland, where she has her palace, perpetually covered with ice. Ask the reindeer who once lived there."

The reindeer answered, "I remember my home, yes, but the Snow Queen's palace is on an island near the North Pole. If she has taken your friend, for sure she will have taken him there."

In the morning, Gerda told the bandit leader's daughter what the doves and the reindeer had said. The young woman ordered the reindeer to conduct Gerda to the Snow Queen's palace. The animal carried Gerda for hours without stopping, through the woods, past the steppes and marshes, going as fast as he could, until they arrived in Lapland. Here they found hospitality with a powerful sorceress, who, after hearing Gerda's story, said, "Little Kay is indeed at the Snow Queen's palace, but he is not a prisoner, at least not in the way you think. He is happy to stay there because there are shards from the devil's mirror in his heart and in one eye," and she explained the story of the mirror.

"The fragments must be removed, otherwise the Snow Queen will retain her power over him forever."

"But can you help Gerda with a potion or an amulet, perhaps?" the reindeer asked.

"I cannot give her a force greater than she already has! She is the only one who can hope to be able to remove the glass from Kay's heart. Two miles from here begins the Snow Queen's garden. Accompany Gerda there and leave her next to a big red berry bush, but hurry back!"

The reindeer galloped off and did not stop until he came to the great bush. There he paused to let the girl dismount, and then he ran away as fast as he could. Alone, Gerda walked through the garden, until suddenly she saw approaching a whole regiment of snowflakes. At least that's how they seemed, for they were not falling from the sky, which was clear and serene. The flakes ran straight into the middle of the garden, getting bigger and bigger, alive and terrifying. They were the soldiers of the Snow Queen and they had the strangest forms. Some looked like horrible hedgehogs, others resembled coiled snakes with their heads poised to strike, still others looked like bears with bristling hair, and all seemed very threatening! Gerda, frightened, began to recite a prayer out loud. The cold was so intense that she could see her breath in front of her. At first, it seemed like smoke, but then it became more dense and turned into small transparent angels which grew larger and larger until they touched the ground. Each one wore a helmet on his head and carried a sword and a shield. In a few instants they had multiplied until they became a whole legion encircling her and protecting her. With their swords, the angels struck out at the snowflakes and sliced them to pieces and so Gerda was able to go on, protected and full of courage, until she reached the Snow Queen's palace. The child entered the palace through a great gate. In front of her there was a grand staircase, its steps cut out of a frozen waterfall. This ascended to the floor above, where there were more than one hundred rooms illuminated by the aurora borealis, all vast, empty, frozen. Right in the middle of the last room there was a frozen lake fragmented into a thousand

pieces, and in the center of this was the Snow Queen's throne and here every day sat little Kay.

The boy's face and hands were purple with cold, but he did not notice. With a kiss, the Snow Queen had seen to it that he did not suffer from the cold. She had made his heart hard as ice and had made him forget everything about his previous life, including his little friend. When Gerda saw him, Kay was sitting at the foot of the throne. He was trying in vain to make the word "eternity" from the fragments around him. The Snow Queen had told him that if he managed to do it he would have become master of himself and she would give him the whole world.

"I have to leave," said the Queen. "I have to go to the warm countries to bring them snow and ice." With that she flew away leaving Kay alone. Now Gerda ran to him and embraced him, but he was immobile, rigid. Little Gerda cried hot tears and these fell on his chest and entered his heart. They melted the block of ice within and corroded away the sliver of mirror that was lodged within. Kay looked at her and then he too burst out crying. He wept so much that the tiny grain of mirror came out of his eye, and now he shouted for joy. "Gerda, where have you been all this time? And where have I been?" he asked, looking around in fright. The scene was so touching that even the fragments of ice began to dance around the pair, forming the letters that the Snow Queen had told Kay to complete, so becoming master of himself and obtaining from her the whole world. The Snow Queen could come back whenever she pleased. The goodbye letter was written there at the foot of the throne in pieces of shimmering ice. The two children joined hands and left the palace, talking without stopping of Kay's grandmother and of the roses on the roof, and where they walked the wind dropped and the sun shone.

When they reached the big red berry bush, they found the reindeer waiting together with another reindeer, his companion.

The two animals carried Kay and Gerda to the borders of their country and here bade them farewell, and soon the children were walking on the path through the woods.

From behind a great oak tree one of the horses that had drawn the golden carriage appeared, ridden by a girl with a red cap on her head and a pair of pistols in her hands. It was the bandit leader's daughter. "Ah, so it was for you that this girl traveled half a world!" she said to Kay. "I hope you're worth the trouble she took!" The two recounted what had happened, and when they had finished, the bandit leader's daughter hugged them tightly and then set off to explore the big wide world.

Little by little as the children got closer to home they saw that spring was bursting forth all around them and they greeted it laughing. When they arrived in their hometown they went to Kay's grandmother's house, ran up the steps and, all smiles, entered the room where nothing had changed. But they had changed. As they crossed the threshold, in fact, they realized that they had grown up! The roses that climbed across the eaves were in flower. Kay and Gerda had already forgotten, as if it were just a bad dream the cold and empty palace of the Snow Queen. They went up to the roses and smiled, and at last the warm summer arrived.

The Tinderbox

A soldier was once marching along the road with a backpack on his back and his sword at his side, on his way home from the war. As he passed through the forest, he came upon an old woman, who said to him, "Would you like a heap of money?"

"Certainly," replied the soldier.

"Do you see that tree?" the woman continued. "It is completely hollow. Climb to the top and then slip down inside. First, I'll tie a rope around your waist, so that I can pull you up again."

"Why do I have to go down into the tree trunk? What will I find there?" asked the soldier.

"A lot of money!" replied the witch. "When you get to the bottom, you will find yourself in a large room illuminated by hundreds of lamps. In front of you, you will see three doors, each with a key in the lock. If you open the first, you come into a room, and in the center you will see a large trunk, on which sits a big dog with eyes as big as saucers. Do not be afraid: spread my apron out on the floor and put the dog on it, then open the chest and take all the coins you want. But, as you will see, they are only copper coins. If you prefer silver, you must go into the second room. There, too, you will find a chest. On this chest sits a dog with eyes as big as millstones. Put him on my apron, and take all the money you want! But if you want gold coins, enter the third room, where you will find a dog with eyes as big as the Round Tower of Copenhagen! Spread my apron on the floor and put him on it. He will give you no trouble and you will be able to take all the gold coins you want!"

"And what do you want in return?" asked the soldier.

"I do not want money. But you must bring me an old tinderbox which my grandmother left there the last time she fell into the tree."

"I promise. Tie the rope around my waist and give me your apron," replied the soldier. He climbed up the tree, then he let himself slide into the trunk, until his feet touched the ground. As the witch had told him, he found himself in a large room. He opened the first door, put the dog on the apron and filled his pockets with copper coins. Then he went into the second room, where he found the second dog, laid him on the apron, got rid of the copper coins and filled his pockets and backpack with silver coins. Then came the third room. The dog that he found there was terrifying, but the soldier laid him on the apron and opened the trunk full of gold coins. He hastily threw away the silver, and filled his pockets, backpack, cap and boots with gold coins. Happy, he closed the trunk, put the dog in his place and called to the witch.

"Have you found the tinderbox?" she asked.

"I forgot, but I'll look for it now!" and he ran to find it.

When the witch pulled him up, the soldier asked her why she wanted the tinderbox, but the old woman told him not to be curious. The soldier threatened her, but the witch would not tell him anything. Then he cut off her head, took the tinderbox back, put the gold in her apron and went to the nearest town. The next day he went to the tailor and bought the most elegant clothes available. The nobility of the region vied to know him, to show him around the city and they told him about the king and his beautiful daughter.

"Where can I go to meet her?" asked the soldier.

"No one can! She lives in a castle surrounded by high walls and towers. The king guards her jealously because according to a prophecy the princess is destined to marry a common soldier, which is for him unthinkable!" they answered.

In the next few days, the soldier continued to enjoy his new life, but money doesn't last forever and he soon found himself with only a few coins in his pocket. So he was forced to move to a miserable attic. One evening, wanting to light a candle, he remembered the tinderbox. He made a spark by striking the flint, and the moment he did so the door flew open and in came the big dog with eyes like saucers.

"What are your orders, master?" he asked.

The soldier ordered the dog to bring him some money. The dog disappeared, to return soon after with a bag full of copper coins. It did not take long before the young man found out how the tinder box worked. If he struck once, the dog who guarded the copper coins appeared. If he struck twice, the dog who had been sitting on the trunk full of silver arrived, and three strikes brought the dog who guarded the trunk full of gold coins. The soldier was thus able to resume his life of luxury. However, there was a thought that he could not get out of his head. He wanted to see the princess at all costs. So, one day he struck the tinderbox and made the dog with eyes as big as saucers appear. He ordered him to fulfill his wish. The dog went off and soon returned with the sleeping princess. She was so beautiful that the young man could not help but kiss her. Then he commanded the dog to take her back to the castle. The following morning the princess told her parents a strange dream she had had, about a dog who had carried her on his back, and a soldier who had kissed her. Suspicious, the king and queen ordered the ladies of the court to keep watch at the princess's bedside. As the previous night, the soldier called the dog and ordered him to bring the princess, but one of the ladies managed to follow him. With a piece of chalk, she drew a cross on the door of the house and returned to the castle. Later, when he was taking the princess back to her bedchamber, the dog saw the cross and he drew the same thing on all the doors of the city, so the next day it was not possible to identify the right one. So, the queen took a bag, filled it with flour, and sewed it to the princess's back. She made a small hole so that the flour would run out along the way. After nightfall, the dog came back to pick up the princess, but this time he did not notice the flour, so the next day it was easy to find the house of the soldier, who was arrested and sentenced to be hanged. The following morning, through the bars of the cell, the poor man saw a large crowd gathering to watch the execution. He was in luck and was able to get the attention of a boy and he asked him to go get the tinderbox from his room in exchange for four coins. Enticed by the reward, the boy obeyed. Meanwhile, the gallows was already erected: the king and queen, counselors and judges came to witness the execution. Once on the scaffold, the soldier addressed the king and queen. "If I am allowed one last wish, I would like to smoke one last pipe."

The king agreed, and the soldier took the tinderbox and struck three times. Suddenly, the three dogs appeared! "Save me!" cried the soldier, and the dogs threw themselves on the judges and the counselors, hurling them so high that there was no escape. The same fate befell the sovereigns. Now everyone present was terrified, and they cried out, "We want you as our king." They hauled him into the king's coach, and, preceded by the three dogs, they went to the royal palace. The princess was very happy to be set free from the castle where her father had imprisoned her and the soldier did not mind either. The wedding was celebrated with great pomp and the two young people lived a long life, happy and content, protected and defended by the three dogs with large eyes.

The Wild Swans

In a distant land, there lived a king with eleven sons and one daughter, Elisa. Their days were serene but their happiness was not to last forever. The father, a widower for many years, in fact, decided to remarry. He chose a very wicked woman, who could not abide the presence of her stepchildren. So, she farmed Elisa out to a family of farmers in the country, and talked so badly about the princes that their father no longer wanted to know them. The queen turned the eleven boys into eleven magnificent wild swans and ordered them to fly away forever. Many years passed, each one sadder than the next. Finally, the princess's fifteenth birthday arrived, and she was brought back to the castle, but as soon as the stepmother saw how beautiful she had become, she began to hate her. At dawn one day she went to the big pool that was the girl's favorite place. She took three toads and ordered the first, "Jump on Elisa's head and make her as stupid as you!" To the second she said, "Jump on her face and make it as ugly and unpleasant as you." Finally, she gave this order to the third toad: "Climb onto her heart and make it so bad that her life is nothing but suffering." Satisfied, she put the three toads in the water. However, things did not go as she had planned. As soon as the three toads came into contact with the girl who was so pure and good, they were transformed into beautiful roses. At the height of her anger, the queen threw herself on Elisa. She smeared her with soot, anointed her with a smelly ointment and matted her hair, until she was unrecognizable, even to her father. Desperate, the princess ran away. She ran without stopping, arriving at last in the woods. She was so tired that she leaned her back against a tree and fell asleep. When she awoke, she bathed in the clear waters of a lake, combed her hair and went on her way. She had not gone far when she met an old woman. Elisa asked her if she had seen eleven princes, and the old woman replied, "I have not

seen eleven princes riding in the woods, but I remember seeing eleven swans with crowns on their heads swimming in the river. If you want, I can take you there."

When they came to the river, the girl thanked the old woman and walked along it, until it ended in a beach. As the sun set, she saw eleven white swans with golden crowns on their heads gliding toward the shore. Elisa, hidden, began to observe them and, when the sun disappeared into the sea, she saw their coats of feathers drop away and they became her brothers. Joyfully, she rushed into their arms, and together they began to laugh and cry. The oldest brother explained that during the day they were swans, but as the sun went down they turned into men. Then he added, "For this reason we always have to take care to be somewhere we can set foot on terra firma at sunset. In fact, if at that time we were still flying in the sky, becoming men, we would fall to our deaths. Now we live in a far country, and only once a year are we allowed to return home. The journey is long. We have to cross the sea and there is only a rock on which we can rest for the night, but it is so small that we barely fit in our human form."

When morning came the princes turned into swans and flew

away, to return after dark and take on human form once more. "Tomorrow we must leave and we cannot return for a year, but we do not want to leave you here! Do you want to come with us?" they asked.

"Yes, indeed, I beg you, take me with you!" exclaimed Elisa.

All night they worked, weaving a net out of willow bark and reeds. When it was ready, Elisa lay on it and her brothers, turning into swans at sunrise, took hold of the net with their beaks, and rose up into the clouds. They flew all day, somewhat slowed by the weight they had to carry. Meanwhile, time was passing fast, and evening was approaching. Anxiously, Elisa watched the sun setting, and the rock was nowhere in sight. Once the sun set, her brothers would become men and fall into the ocean. The sun was on the horizon. Elisa's heart trembled, then, finally, she saw the tiny rock. Her foot touched the it just as the sun disappeared into the sea. Elisa looked around and saw that her brothers were holding her in their hands. The following day, at dawn, the swans continued their flight. As the sun rose higher, Elisa saw before her a mountain hanging in the air. Glaciers glittered among the rocks and in the center stood a magnificent castle, surrounded by imposing colonnades, and by forests of palm trees and beautiful flowers. Elisa asked if this was their new home, but the swans shook their heads. What she was seeing was Morgan le Fay's ever-changing castle of clouds. The journey continued for an age, but just before sunset, Elisa found herself on a rock hidden behind creepers.

"I wonder what we will dream tonight!" said the youngest of the brothers.

"I wish I could dream how to save you!" said the girl, then, exhausted, she fell asleep. She seemed to fly up to Morgan le Fay's castle of clouds.

She saw the enchantress come to meet her, beautiful and sparkling, and yet so much like the old woman she met in the forest.

"You can save your brothers, but you must be very strong and tenacious, because you will have to endure much pain and face many fears," said the fairy. "See these nettles? They grow near the cave where you are sleeping or among the graves of the cemetery. You will need to pick them and even if they burn your skin horribly, make them into yarn, and from the yarn weave eleven tunics. Throw the tunics over the eleven swans. This is the only way to break the spell. But remember, from the moment you start work, even though it may take years, you must no longer speak. A single word will bring about your brothers' death!"

When she awoke, Elisa found nettles next to her bed. She left the cave and began her work. The nettles stung the skin of her hands and arms, but she did not stop. She trod each nettle plant with her bare feet, so producing the yarn she needed for her weaving. When her brothers saw what she was doing, they were frightened for her, but then they realized that she was paying the price for their salvation. Elisa worked all night and managed to finish one tunic. Suddenly, she heard the blast of hunting horns and the barking of dogs. Terrified, she took refuge in the cave, taking with her the nettles she had collected. A short time later, the hunters appeared. Among them was the king of that distant country. The young man entered the cave and was stopped short by the sight of Elisa. He had never seen such a beautiful girl!

"Where are you from?" he asked. Elisa shook her head without saying a word.

"Come with me!" the king told her, "You will be my queen." And so saying, he made her get on his horse and they rode off toward the royal palace. Disconsolate, Elisa wept throughout the ride, without being able to say anything. At the castle, the ladies dressed her in royal clothes, adorned her with beautiful jewels and covered the wounds on her hands with soft gloves. Elisa looked gorgeous! The king introduced her to everyone as his future bride, but she did not smile and she never spoke a word. Then the king opened the door of a room near Elisa's bedroom.

On the floor she saw the threads she had extracted from the nettles and the one tunic she had finished. As soon as she saw them, Elisa smiled and kissed the king's hand. Despite the opposition of the archbishop, who suspected the future queen of witchcraft, the marriage was celebrated with great solemnity. The king loved his wife, but could not understand her behavior. Every night, the young woman left him and went into her private room, where she wove one tunic after another. She had already completed six, when she ran out of material. The enchantress had told her that the nettles she must use grew in the cemetery, so she decided to go there as soon as night fell. Unfortunately, the archbishop saw her and tried to convince the king that his suspicions were well founded. Many more days and nights passed, and the young woman had almost finished her work, but she once again found she had run out of nettles. Reluctantly, she decided to return to the cemetery. This time, however, the king and the archbishop followed her. Faced with the evidence, the king could not do anything and Elisa was brought before the court, tried for witchcraft and condemned to die at the stake. She was taken to prison and as bedding they gave her the rough nettle tunics. She began working immediately, still in silence, and without any way of explaining or defending himself. Towards evening, her brothers arrived. This was perhaps the last time she would see them, but the work was almost finished and they were close to her. She had just one more night to finish the last shirt. Desperate, the eleven brothers asked to be received by the king. They threatened and begged, but there was nothing to be done, and as the sun rose again they became swans. All the people flocked to the city to see the burning of

the witch. Elisa arrived on a cart, dressed in a shabby cloth tunic: not even then did the girl stop sewing. The people insulted her and some rushed at her to take away the work that seemed to be so important to her, thinking it must be part of an evil spell. Then, from above, came eleven swans, and they surrounded the cart, beating the crowd away with their wings. The people fled in terror. The executioner managed to grab Elisa's hand, but now she was hurriedly throwing eleven tunics over the swans. The creatures immediately changed into their human form. The youngest, however, bore a wing instead of an arm. His sister had not had time to finish his tunic.

"Elisa is innocent!" cried the eldest brother and told the whole story. Moved, the people bowed down in front of her as if she were a saint. Freed from her oath, the girl was able to explain everything to her husband and to tell him she loved him and forgave him for having suspected her. From that day on they all lived happily together at the castle, far away from their sad memories.

The Nightingale

The emperor of China's palace was the most beautiful in the world, entirely built from the finest porcelain. The garden was wonderful as well. Silver bells had been attached to each flower and they tinkled gently in the wind and the garden was so vast that it was impossible to come to the end of it. If you continued to walk for a long time, you would come to a beautiful forest with tall trees and crystal-clear pools. The forest ran down to the sea, so travelers, sailors and fishermen could sail in the shade of the trees, listening, enraptured, to the melodious song of a nightingale who lived among the leafy branches. Though enchanted by the splendor and wealth of the royal palace, everyone who visited talked about nothing but the nightingale when they returned home. The talk reached the ears of the emperor who called his lieutenant and his counselors and asked about this wonder, but none of them knew anything. Annoyed, the emperor ordered the nightingale to be brought to court immediately. The lieutenant asked everywhere for news of the melodious bird and finally, just as he had begun to despair and fear imperial punishment, he found a young girl in the kitchen who said, "I know the nightingale. She lives near the beach and sings divinely."

So everyone made their way into the woods, and when the girl finally pointed to a bird perched on a branch, the lieutenant, a little disappointed by her dull appearance, addressed her solemnly, "Little nightingale, our great emperor wishes you to sing for him!"

"Gladly," said the nightingale, and filled the air with her wonderful melodies.

The lieutenant, shaking off the music's enchantment, announced, "I have the pleasure of inviting you to a celebration this evening at court, where you will delight our beloved sovereign with your singing!"

At the palace, great preparations for the evening were under way. All the courtiers in their sumptuous clothes were present, and in the middle of the great hall, next to the emperor's throne, a golden perch was placed for the nightingale. She sang so well that night that the even the emperor was moved to tears, and he decided that from that day the bird would remain at court, in a golden cage. She would be permitted to fly twice a day and once at night, but tied to twelve silk ribbons held by twelve servants. One day, a large parcel was brought to the emperor, on which was written: "NIGHTINGALE". Inside was a small nightingale, but it was mechanical and was covered with diamonds, rubies and sapphires. As soon as it was wound up, it began to sing, moving its golden tail. Around its neck was a ribbon, on which was written: "The emperor of China's nightingale is a poor thing compared to that of the emperor of Japan." Everyone was enchanted, and the emperor desired that the two birds, the real one and the one mechanical one, would sing together in a beautiful duet.

Actually, things did not go very well, so they had them sing separately. Both were very good, but the mechanical nightingale received greater acclaim since it was also so beautiful to look at, as it sparkled with gold and precious stones. It sang thirty-three times, and always the same melody, always perfectly, and people would gladly have heard it again, but the emperor declared his desire to hear the real nightingale... but where was she? Seduced as they were by the song of the mechanical nightingale, they had not realized that the bird had flown out the window, toward the woods.

After a moment of surprise and dismay, they all agreed that, after all, the mechanical nightingale was far better than the real thing, and they proceeded to listen to the same melody for the thirty-fourth time.

The master of the emperor's music got permission to show the bird to the people. Thus, the following Sunday, everyone listened and praised the song of the mechanical nightingale. Everyone, that is, except the fishermen who had been lucky enough to enjoy the melodies of the real bird, and they did not find the mechanical bird's performance so very impressive. The real nightingale was banished from the empire, and the artificial bird was placed on a silk cushion close to the emperor's bed, and was awarded the title of 'Imperial Singer'. So, a year passed, and the emperor, his courtiers and all the Chinese learned by heart every note of the artificial bird's song and sang it all the time.

One evening, while the artificial bird was singing for the emperor as he lay in his beautiful royal bed, it produced a strange metallic sound, and then the music stopped altogether. The emperor sprang out of bed, and called his doctor, who could do nothing. Then he called the watchmaker, who with great difficulty somehow repaired the bird, but said that the emperor must use it as little as possible because its parts were now worn out and he could not replace them. With great regret, the emperor decreed that he would listen to the mechanical bird only once a year, in order to preserve its song.

Five years passed, and the whole country was deeply saddened by the state of health of their beloved emperor, who was seriously ill. He would not live much longer, and a new ruler had already been chosen. One terrible night, the valets found the emperor pale and cold in his big bed. Believing him dead, they ran to hail the new emperor. In the sumptuous halls and corridors of the royal palace, the floors were covered with heavy carpets, so that every noise was muffled and silence reigned everywhere.

The emperor, however, was not dead yet. The window of his room was open, allowing the silvery light of the moon to fall on him and on the precious mechanical nightingale.

The emperor was breathing with difficulty and now saw death, who, sitting on his chest, wore a gold crown on his head, resplendent with precious stones. In one hand he held a golden sword and in the other a beautiful banner. Around them, among the folds of the heavy velvet curtains, strange figures appeared, some frightening, some sweet and tender; they were the emperor's actions, both good and bad, and they were watching him now that death was imminent.

"Do you remember?" they whispered one after the other.

"Do you remember?" And they told him so many things, so many evil deeds and so many injustices that the emperor had committed but which he did not even recall. He was so frightened that sweat ran from his frozen forehead and he asked with the little voice he had left, "Music! I want the music of the great Chinese drum! I don't want to hear what they are saying!"

But the strange figures continued without mercy and death nodded his head, confirming everything they said.

"Music! Music!" shouted the emperor in desperation. "And you, my beloved golden nightingale, sing, sing as loud as you can! I have conferred on you the highest honors. I have always kept you next to me. So, sing, sing now!"

But the bird was silent, because there was no one to wind it up.

Death continued to loom silent and ominous above the emperor, looking at him with his horrible hollow orbits, brandishing the sword with one hand and holding his banner with the other.

At that moment, from the window came a marvelous song, and it spread throughout the room. It was the little nightingale of the woods who had heard from the fishermen of the great suffering that afflicted the emperor and had come to comfort him with her melodies and give him new hope. While she was singing, the disturbing shapes, peeping from the folds of the curtains, grew paler and paler, and their voices grew increasingly distant. The blood began to flow more strongly in the exhausted body of the emperor, giving him renewed vigor.

Even death listened to the sweet song in admiration, and he encouraged her not to stop, but to prolong her song with melodies that were ever new. "Go on, little Nightingale, go on," he said.

"Only if you give me your golden sword, and your rich banner. Only if you give me the emperor's crown!" replied the nightingale.

And death, without hesitation, gave her everything she asked for or in exchange for another song. The nightingale went on singing. She sang of the quiet churchyard where white roses were blooming, where the elder tree's perfume was delicate, where the grass was watered by the tears of those who mourned the loss of loved-ones. Then, death, assailed by a deep longing for his garden, floated like white fog out of the window. The emperor thanked the nightingale and told her, "My little friend, I imprisoned you and then I banished you from my kingdom, and yet you came to my rescue. You charmed away from my bed those evil visions, and you have driven death from my heart. How can I reward you? Ask me anything and it shall be yours!"

"I already have my reward," said the nightingale. "You gave me your tears the first time I sang to you: remember? I will never forget it! But now rest and get well. I will stay beside you and sing for you."

The following morning, when he woke up, the emperor was healed and full of energy. "Stay with me forever!" he begged the nightingale. "You shall sing only when it pleases you, and I will destroy the mechanical bird."

"Do not do it," said the nightingale. "Keep it with you. I cannot live in the palace, but I will come every night and sing for you, to give you the serenity to think of the good you can do for those who suffer and how you can remedy the injustices that are committed without your knowledge. I will come to sing for you, but you have to promise me something."

"Whatever you desire!" replied the emperor.

"Never tell anyone that I come every day to tell you what is happening in your kingdom." So saying, the nightingale flew away.

The emperor's servants entered the emperor's bedchamber that morning, believing him dead. Imagine their astonishment when he greeted them with a cheerful "Good morning!"

Thumbelina

There was once a woman who longed to have a child, but having lost all hope, she decided to resort to the magical arts of an old witch. So, she went to her to ask if she could help her realize her dream. "It is not complicated!" said the witch. "Here is a grain of barley. But mind, this is not a common grain such as those you give to the chickens. Plant it in a pot and you'll see that your wish will come true." After paying the old witch with the twelve coins they had agreed on, and having thanked her, she went home and planted the grain of barley in a beautiful pot. It was not long before a lovely flower appeared, like a tulip, but with its petals tightly closed. The woman was admiring it one day when, suddenly, she felt a tiny explosion and the petals opened up, revealing within them a very small girl child, very delicate and very graceful. Imagine the woman's surprise! In admiration, she looked closer at the child. She was no taller than a thumb, so the woman decided to call her Thumbelina.

She took a walnut shell and made it into a cradle, decorating it with colored patterns, making a mattress out of purple leaves and adding a rose petal as a cover. During the day, the girl played on the table, where the woman had placed a plate, which she had filled with water and decorated with fragrant flowers around the edge. A tulip petal served as a boat, and it amused Thumbelina to sail in it on the lake with the help of two horse hairs which she used as oars. It was a truly enchanting sight, and the child made it even more moving as she sang with a sweet and melodious voice. The days passed in complete serenity, and the woman felt happier than she had ever been in her life.

But one terrible night a big, slimy toad jumped in through the window and saw Thumbelina asleep in her walnut shell.

The toad was enchanted and thought Thumbelina would make the perfect bride for her son. So, she took the child as she slept, cradle and all, and returned to the pond at the bottom of the garden. The toad's son was just as ugly and slimy as his mother, and when he saw Thumbelina he croaked happily but in a most inelegant way: "Ribbet! Ribbet!" His mother scolded him: "Don't shout, you might wake her up and frighten her away. Let's put her nutshell on this big lily pad in the middle of the pond, surrounded by water, so that she cannot escape, while we go and prepare your new home."

The following morning, when she awoke, the girl looked around bewildered, unable to figure out where he was. Frightened, she began to cry and tried in vain to find some way of escaping, but around her there was nothing but the dark water of the pond. Meanwhile, the mother toad and her son had completed their preparations. Now they saw that she was awake and swam to the leaf on which Thumbelina was crying desperately. Trying her best to soothe her, the mother toad said, "This is my son, your future husband. You will go and live with him at the bottom of the pond in the beautiful house we have prepared for you." Saying this, the two toads began to draw Thumbelina towards her new home. Meanwhile, the fish in the pond had witnessed the scene, and, curious about the new bride, they began to crowd around the leaf on which the little girl was still weeping. As soon as they saw her, they were enchanted by her grace and decided to help her escape this horrible fate. Quick as a flash, they swam down to the bottom of the pond and with their teeth began to saw at the stem of the lily until at last, freed of its anchor, it began to float across the water, carrying Thumbelina

away from her kidnappers. Now the little girl embarked on a long journey, cheered by the chirping of birds and accompanied by a lovely butterfly. To navigate more quickly, Thumbelina tied one end of her belt to the stem of the leaf and the other to the butterfly's waist. Soon, however, her journey was interrupted. A huge beetle, dived down on the child and, grabbing her with his feet, carried her away to a tree, while the lily pad floated on its way, taking the poor butterfly with it, still attached to its stem by the belt. Scared and desperate for her friend, Thumbelina lay on the highest leaf of the tree. The beetle brought her some pollen and then settled down to look at her. He was perplexed, for in her he could not see any resemblance to his own race. Other beetles arrived, and they all began to examine her carefully. "But it has only two legs," said one. "And it doesn't have any the antennas," noted another. "And not even wings!" exclaimed a third. "It's really ugly!" concluded a fourth. So, the beetle, while finding Thumbelina so pretty, was persuaded to give her up and he carried her to the foot of the tree, and deposited her on a daisy. All summer long the child lived alone in the woods, eating flower pollen and drinking the morning dew, but the summer passed quickly, and autumn came, and then came the winter. Now it was cold, it rained often and sometimes falling snowflakes were so big that they covered her completely. Thumbelina could not always find anything to eat, and dry leaves were not enough to keep her warm. Although she was by now weak, the girl decided to cross the vast wheat field - now frozen - that stretched out beyond the forest, to seek help. Thus, she came to the house of a little field mouse, who lived in a hole dug under the stubble. The house was very comfortable. There was a big kitchen, a cozy living room and an ample pantry full of grain. Thumbelina knocked on the door, and asked politely for something to eat. The little mouse was immediately enchanted by the girl's grace and told

her she could stay until winter's end, provided she would help her with the housework and tell good stories. Thumbelina accepted happily. One day she went to visit an old friend of the little mouse. It was Mr. Mole, who lived in a beautiful house close by. It had large rooms, an elegant lounge and a pantry full of food. In short, it was a party not to be missed! Mr. Mole, who could not see anything and who hated the sun and light, made a fine show of his soft black fur. He made sure they knew how wealthy he was and did his best to show off his wide knowledge. The little mouse asked Thumbelina to sing something, and Mr. Mole, hearing her sweet voice, fell in love with the girl. He told them he had just dug a tunnel that passed from his home to that of the little mouse and he invited them to visit whenever they wished. He added that they should not be frightened by the presence of a dead bird, which was harmless. Then he offered to accompany them, going ahead to show them the way. Reaching the dead bird, Mr. Mole made a hole in the ceiling of the tunnel to let a little light in. On the floor lay a poor, lifeless swallow. Thumbelina felt great pity for her, while their companion gave her a violent kick. That night the little girl could not sleep for thinking about the poor swallow, so she got up and ventured into the tunnel, taking with her some straw to cover it and keep it warm. As she stooped to stroke the soft feathers, Thumbelina felt the bird's heart beating feebly: the swallow was still alive! Thumbelina took care of her all winter. Secretly, she took her food and water, and healed the wound that she had received when she had fallen among the brambles, and which had prevented her from flying with her companions to warmer places at the end of the summer.

When spring came, the little girl opened the hole that Mr. Mole had made in the ceiling and freed her friend. The swallow offered to carry her away on her back, but Thumbelina was grateful to the little mouse and did not want to leave her alone. So, the swallow flew away. The little mouse, for her

part, had big plans for the little girl. She had decided that she should be given in marriage to Mr. Mole, and had already begun to make her trousseau. Thumbelina really did not want to, and often she gazed at the sky, hoping to see her friend the swallow. Autumn came and with it came their wedding day. The child was very sad. She could look forward to a life of boredom and darkness! She decided to say a final farewell to the sun and the light, and she went out into the open air, savoring the last few minutes of joy. It was at that moment that she heard the unmistakable fluttering of a swallow. It was her friend who, after listening to her story, asked her to fly away with her. This time without hesitation, Thumbelina sat on the back of the swallow and flew away with her toward the south. They crossed many wonderful lands and eventually stopped near a lake, on whose shores stood a magnificent marble palace. This was their destination. Here the swallow had her nest. She put Thumbelina down on a large lily and said goodbye. With amazement the little girl saw a little man, sitting on a flower. He was all white, transparent as glass. He had a shiny crown on his head and from his shoulders protruded two beautiful mother-of-pearl wings. It was the king of the lilies and all the tiny people who lived among them. The two fell in love at first sight and decided to get married. The day of the wedding, Thumbelina received as a gift two beautiful wings, which allowed her to fly freely from flower to flower. She was also given a new name: Maia. After the wedding, the swallow came to greet the new queen of lilies and then flew off to distant shores, bringing to the world the extraordinary story of Thumbelina.

Francesca Rossi

Born in 1983, she graduated from the International School of Comics in Florence. She publishes illustrated books with various Italian publishers and does drawings for covers and posters. In addition to illustrating, she offers educational workshops in schools and libraries, and creates and decorates ceramic art. In the past years, she has illustrated several books for White Star Kids, with great enthusiasm and creativity.

WSkids
WHITE STAR KIDS

White Star Kids® is a registered trademark property of White Star s.r.l.

© 2018 White Star s.r.l.
Piazzale Luigi Cadorna, 6 - 20123 Milan, Italy
www.whitestar.it

Translation and Editing: Contextus Srl, Pavia
(translation: Louise Bostock, Aubrey Lawrence)

ISBN 978-88-544-1257-6
2 3 4 5 6   22 21 20 19 18

Printed in China